Books by Ralph McInerny

Connolly's Life   1983
Romanesque   1978
Spinnaker   1977
Rogerson at Bay   1976
Gate of Heaven   1975
The Priest   1973
A Narrow Time   1969
Jolly Rogerson   1967

The Father Dowling Mystery Series

A Loss of Patients   1982
Thicker Than Water   1981
Second Vespers   1980
Lying Three   1979
Bishop as Pawn   1978
The Seventh Station   1977
Her Death of Cold   1976

Connolly's Life

Connolly's Life

Ralph McInerny

Atheneum   New York   1983

Library of Congress Cataloging in Publication Data

McInerny, Ralph M.
Connolly's life.

I. Title.
PS3563.A31166C6   1983   813'.54   82-73021
ISBN 0-689-11356-0

Published simultaneously in Canada by McClelland & Stewart Ltd.
Composed by Maryland Linotype Composition Company,
Baltimore, Maryland
Manufactured by Fairfield Graphics, Fairfield, Pennsylvania
Designed by Mary Cregan
First Edition

For Guy and Sally Norton
with thanks for the use of the Abbey

"For whoever after having been dead awakens to the same life was merely in a trance."

—Johannes Climacus

Part One

Chapter 1

When I think of all the names of cardinals lettered across the facades of churches in this city as testimony to their restorative ardor, I wonder if Connolly is content now with the more fleeting immortality he won for his efforts to bring the Holy Roman Catholic Church into the mainstream of the twentieth century. If Keats's name was writ in water, Connolly's was writ in ink, his own and others', over a period of twenty years. He was one of the new breed of theologian intent on taunting bishops and popes with his version of Vatican II. He was the darling of the avant-garde: innovative, daring, subversive. And he was a sonofabitch.

Perhaps a more fitting local symbol of him would be the

hooded brooding figure of Giordano Bruno high on his pedestal among the fish stalls in the Campo di Fiori.

The news that any further talk of Connolly must be in the past tense came when Maria and I were lunching at the Otello. April sunlight filtered through the already burgeoning branches of vines trained on a latticework over the tables. Maria frowned at the English language paper while I read *Il Tempo*. I had ordered white wine, cannelloni and a salad. After we ate we would go on to the Caffè Greco for coffee. How swiftly life becomes routine. At my age that is welcome, but Maria was growing bored. I had promised to take her to the Amalfi coast as soon as I finished my current book, and it was the prospect of the trip that made life bearable for her.

She had arrived in Rome the previous September to do her junior year at Loyola. Product of a broken home, survivor of an affair with one of her professors in Chicago, she was spoiled, neurotic and irresistible. Her lips moved as she read, she twisted a strand of hair in the long-nailed fingers of one hand, the other gently surrounding the stem of her glass. Her paper was propped against our liter of wine as if she were making a special claim on it. She drank too much. She did everything to excess. For me she was both good luck and bad.

I had met her in a cellar restaurant off the Via Monterone to which I had come early, not realizing it was a student haunt. And then they arrived, dozens of them. Tables were moved and rearranged, the proprietor became animated, his waiters wary, and I found myself uncomfortably afloat in a sea of youth. Maria wore cream-colored slacks and a blue velour blouse with a deep V neck. At first she ignored me, though our chairs kept bumping as she settled in. I was struck by the reckless way she tossed off her wine. Her companion was a redhead, sullen and silent, who seemed resentful of the fun she was having. She half stood to reach

4

for a carafe, her chair hit my elbow and acqua minerale splashed in my lap.

"My God, I'm sorry," she cried and then, seeing the damage, laughed.

The accident and the laughter should have annoyed me, but they did not. She angled her chair around, helped herself to my wine, and asked what I was doing in Rome. The fact that I lived there rescued me from the status of tourist. The annoyance of her frowning companion flattered me, and I felt she was enlisting me in a childish game when she asked for my address and telephone number. Later, when she phoned and asked if I remembered her, I could not pretend that I did not.

Maria fitted a pattern that has become too familiar: the resentful daughter despising parents who had learned to despise one another and inevitably parted. Her father had remarried, his new wife scarcely older than Maria. She apparently did not see how exactly we matched the pair she found disgusting. Her mother shared an apartment with another woman. She was liberated now. Could lesbianism be far behind? Maria was obsessed by the possibility.

"There's more of that now, isn't there?" Her voice was a warm murmur on my bare chest, her arm lay across my body like the bar sinister, my shoulder in the grip of her hand.

"So they say."

There was a long silence. "It should disgust me but it doesn't."

"Have you ever . . ."

She shook her head slowly, and her hair against my flesh put me in mind of a poem by Donne. It is the cross of the hack writer to be visited constantly by thoughts of his betters. For years I had been writing juvenile fiction under a platoon of pseudonyms.

5

We lay on my wide bed, only a sheet over us, the great double windows of the room open so that we could look out over the rooftops of Rome as at a picture framed for our viewing. It was midafternoon, the second or third time we had been together. Maria was complaining about her student residence in the suburbs.

"You don't have to live there, do you?"

"I've stopped going to class."

I checked the impulse to tell her what I thought of her education. The more people exposed to higher learning, the lower it gets.

"Where could I live?"

"With me."

A casual suggestion, casually accepted. I did not search the moment for omens and portents. Years before, when I quit smoking, I had felt I was conferring immortality on myself. Now I would never die. When Maria moved in with me I felt I had returned to the threshold of life and become as young as she. But the moment, like all moments, could be negated. I had stopped acquiring a history.

She brought with her youth, enthusiastic curiosity about the old city, sex and, finally, boredom. "What are we going to do today?" was her morning question, and if at first I welcomed her love of Rome, I soon grew weary of the role of guide and missed the time when I had gone from breakfast to my typewriter without concern for wishes other than my own. For her I represented, I suppose, a species of revenge. She used me to thumb her nose at the remarried father in Evanston and the mother sharing an apartment with a questionable lady in a round tower overlooking the Chicago River. And I also served to tease Austin, her sullen companion of the night we met.

In the Otello, she poured herself another glass of wine,

and her paper slid flat upon the table. Connolly's name, upside down, caught my eye. I took the paper.

How dispassionately I read the story of Michael Connolly's death. I might have been catching up on the scores of soccer games that had not interested me in the first place. Or so I thought. Maria noticed something.

"What is it?"

"Someone I know has died."

"Who?"

I showed her the story and she said, "Oh, did you know him? He lectured to us once." She meant at the campus in suburban Chicago. "The faculty was delirious, especially those in religious studies."

"What did you think of him?"

She thought for a moment. "I don't remember." I doubted that would be Mike Connolly's epitaph. "Where did you know him, Jim?"

"It's a long story."

A long story indeed, as long as my life. Michael Connolly, boyhood friend, priest, controversial theologian, sonofabitch, was dead.

Chapter 2

Two hours later Maria and I sat at a table outside a café in Fiumicino, come a roundabout way from lunch. She was drinking a Birra Pironi while I opened the package of cigarettes I had bought.

"You don't smoke," Maria said.

"I know."

"What's the matter, Jim?"

How could anything be the matter? Gulls swept overhead, the fishy smell of the sea rode the breeze that tossed her hair and caused her, despite the sun, to draw her sweater over her shoulders.

I took a cigarette from the packet, and the feel of it in

my fingers was both odd and familiar, a tactile memory that went back more than seven years. It was still an open question whether or not I would smoke it. I had bought a box of *cerini*, a hundred wax-covered miniature matches. The wind blew out the first two before I could get them to the tip of the cigarette, as if Nature or God or the Life Force were bent on preventing me from doing injury to myself. When at last the cigarette was lit and the taste of smoke tart upon my tongue, Maria put down her beer and shook her head.

"That's stupid."

"I know."

Under the indirect tutelage of theologians like Connolly, Maria found most moral questions ambiguous, easily solved in favor of one's desires, but she was not devoid of ethical absolutes, and the prohibition on smoking was a maxim admitting no exceptions. At Newman Hall Connolly and I had sneaked cigarettes in the woods around the school. Chesterfields. The Italian MS I smoked that April afternoon brought back sharp memories of springtime mud, the smell of rotting humus, the sound of a stream swollen with melted snow. Wisconsin thirty years ago. Overhead now a jet settled down toward Leonardo da Vinci airport.

"You've been working too hard," Maria said. She was seeking an explanation for my smoking. "Let's go to Amalfi now. You can bring your typewriter along."

"How would you like to go to the States instead?"

"You're kidding."

"Pan Am has a flight in the morning that will take us right into Dulles."

"I do not want to go to the States."

I was counting on that. My decision to go home had been made at the Otello, and with it Maria became a problem. I had no intention of taking a twenty-year-old girl with

9

me, mocking the pilgrimage this flight into the past would be. One look at Maria would give Nancy a moral authority I did not care to confer on her.

"Why did we come here?"

Maria shivered in the sunlight and looked with distaste up and down the street. All the buildings were on one side. Opposite was a canal leading to the sea. In the distance, a freighter made inching progress southward. The rusty sight of it awakened old desires. Some years before, I was a frequent passenger on such ships, their destination mine, wanting only the peace of suspended time in which to work. My writing has always gone well on boats. Connolly had been fascinated when I told him of life aboard a freighter, good food, unusual fellow passengers, people going nowhere like myself. He resolved to subscribe to *Ford's Freighter Guide*. I wondered if he ever did. It would be of no use to him now. He had crossed the Styx in Charon's boat.

"To enjoy the sea," I told Maria.

"It smells." She wrinkled her nose. "Are you going home?"

She meant the States. I no longer regarded it as home. "Yes."

"Because of Father Connolly?"

"Yes."

"Did you know him that well?"

Her manner was receptive. No doubt the prospect of my absence had its attraction. Speculative thoughts altered the focus of her eyes. Alone in Rome. She could remain in my apartment without the boredom of my work. Did Austin enter into her fantasies?

"Too well to ignore his death."

"Where will the funeral be?"

"He was a native of Wisconsin."

"Like you."

"Like me."

On the way to the airport, where I booked a seat on the morning flight to Washington, Maria suffered my reminiscing about Connolly, her interest a down payment on the excitement lying before her. Would she hang around the Piazza Navona and fall in with addicts? I had forbidden her to smoke marijuana in my apartment. I lost interest in discussing Connolly with her.

It was always difficult for us to come up with topics of shared interest. Outside of bed. Bed was the great equalizer. There, relative inexperience gives its own kind of advantage. It certainly whets the appetite. In bed with her I could imagine myself Horace with his Lalage, sweetly laughing, sweetly talking. The old pagan poet in his retreat above Tivoli had certainly not talked shop with his nubile concubine.

Yet for the rest of the day we talked endlessly, neither of us shutting up; there was so much we did not want to talk about. Late in the afternoon, I picked up a copy of *L'Osservatore Romano*, the Vatican paper. There was no mention of Connolly. Perhaps someone was preparing a retrospective essay in lieu of an obituary. Now a final assessment, and condemnation, of Connolly could be made without fear of his rebuttal.

I walked to St. Peter's Square to buy the paper and looked up over the Bernini colonnade at the windows of the papal apartments. Did the man in the white cassock know of Connolly's death? Il Papa Polacco had proved to be more adroit and formidable than Connolly had imagined. John Paul's trips around the globe to rally the faithful threatened to undo the chaos theologians had created. Connolly went on the attack. When he was summoned to Rome, the confrontation had not taken place in the Vatican. America's most famous dissident theologian had faced his inquisitors in the Palazzo della Cancelleria, just around the corner from my apartment.

"Jim," he said, after the first meeting, sprawling on my couch, a Scotch on the rocks tinkling in his hand, "they are absolutely Neanderthal. No, I take that back. They would bristle at the mention of Neanderthal man. They are fundamentalists. There is no other word for them."

"How about Catholics?"

"They don't know the meaning of the word. They're provincial. They still think Rome is the center of the action."

"And they believe Jesus really rose from the dead."

He made a face over the rim of his glass and drank. The clerical clothes he wore in deference to the occasion struck me as an unworthy concession. But his hair, gone white, was even more dramatic in black clerical attire. The alligator loafers with their silver ornaments were a nice touch, however, doubtless noticed by his interrogators. Bogus buskins. The topic of discussion was Connolly's little book on the Resurrection.

I said, "Why don't you just admit that you no longer believe what they believe? They want you to admit that Jesus literally walked out of his grave and was seen in the flesh by lots of people."

"Who oddly did not recognize him."

"You see? You're skeptical. But that is what Christians have believed for two thousand years."

"Jimmy, Jimmy, not you too."

"*Et tu, Brute*? You're in the right town for that complaint. Where shall we eat?"

"I am hungry. You'd think someone who had been fed to the lions would lose his appetite."

"Maybe you're the lion."

He liked that. Well, who is not susceptible to flattery?

The truth was that I sided with Connolly's accusers. I wanted to be as clear as possible about the content of the faith I had repudiated. Connolly would let me go on reciting the Creed and not mean a word of it.

"Let's not argue. I've spent the day arguing."

When we parted after dinner, he said, "I don't expect to persuade them, Jim. This is just for the record."

"The Book of Life?"

"Maybe."

More likely *Time*. When Connolly was not with me, he was with reporters, briefing them on the events of the day, getting his side of the proceedings into print. This was a breach of the ground rules, but then the other side kept *L'Osservatore Romano* posted. It was an old story by then, theological controversy conducted in the public press. Connolly had done as much as anyone to bring about that revolution when he was in Rome as correspondent for a liberal agnostic New York weekly during the Council. We had tried unsuccessfully to get him to write for *Alleluia*, but he had thought that even our tenuous connections with the official Church would prove too much of a constraint.

It had been my idea to hire him as our man at the Council—not that Gilligan, the editor, had needed persuading. *Alleluia*'s loss was my gain since, in the end, it was I who was sent to Rome to cover the Council. Bliss was it in that dawn to be alive. Nancy and I lived in a little hotel near the Piazza Cavour, on the sixth floor, our balcony providing us with a striking view of the great dome of St. Peter's looking for all the world like the sun rising from the jumble of the intervening buildings.

"More likely setting," Nancy said.

It was the most frequent subject of the watercolors she was attempting. When I came home from the Vatican, she would be out on the balcony daubing away. She would turn and squint into the room when she heard me come in,

1 3

but the sunlight blinded her. On the sweatshirt she wore was the name of her college, Maris Stella. She smoked two packs of Nazionales a day, stubbing them out on the concrete floor of the balcony and then, with a flick of the finger, sending them cartwheeling into space. Her ash-blond hair was long then, usually pulled back into a pony-tail when she worked. Nancy had been a postulant in one of the lesser varieties of the Franciscan Order before coming to *Alleluia*. Her wide-set blue eyes and Slavic cheek-bones seemed to underscore her receptiveness to the world she had once thought of putting behind her. My long-standing friendship with Connolly increased my impor-tance in her eyes, and I had no compunction in taking advantage of the reflected glamour. We were married in a little church a few blocks from Grand Central, the Rever-end Michael Connolly officiating. "Michael Connolly mar-ried us," Nancy loved to say, a locution that, however odd, seemed borne out by the way the three of us hung together in Rome during the Council. The *aggiornamento* of Nancy's life still had a long way to go. She was recovering from her lost vocation and our lost child and would go on eventually to have the marriage Michael Connolly wit-nessed annulled.

A figure in bib overalls, a T-shirt and unmistakable red hair loitered in the street outside my apartment when I returned. Austin. He pushed away from the wall he had been leaning against when I came up.

"Clark," he said, an identification and a greeting. His eyes had the too bright look of the stoned.

"Austin, isn't it?"

"I want to talk with you about Maria." He stopped, apparently forgetting a speech he had prepared.

"You've picked a bad time. I'm leaving for the States in the morning."

"Is Maria going with you?"

"Certainly not."

My surprised tone was meant to deceive him, I suppose, but it also expressed my true feelings. The episode with Maria, like others before it, was at an end. All that remained was the formal leave-taking, and I did not want to get involved in that now. After I returned, the saving interlude of my absence would make it easier. Nonetheless, I resented Austin's proprietary air.

"Wouldn't it make more sense if you talked with her?"

"Where the hell is she?"

That meant he did not know she was in my apartment. "I couldn't tell you."

He clenched and unclenched his fists and his mouth worked. What is more pitiful than a man who desires a woman of whom one has tired? I no longer felt any sense of triumph that Maria had preferred me to Austin. He gave me a malevolent look, turned and walked rapidly away. Going up in the elevator to Maria, I had a sharp realization of the futility of the life I led.

Chapter 3

In the morning, with freedom imminent, Maria was a model of busy helpfulness and would have driven me to the airport if I had not insisted that I wanted to take the bus from the train station. She could drop me there. The thought of her returning alone on the crazy racecourse of the Via del Mare, where anything less than 140 kph is considered slow, was not one I wanted to carry with me on the flight. It was bad enough to think of her driving in the city, Roman traffic being the Demolition Derby it is. My concern was not for my secondhand Fiat, whose fenders already bore the marks of battle. An accident, even if Maria brazened out the impromptu drama a collision invariably led to, could mean endless legal wrangling, bound to prove expensive for me. Besides, Maria had no driver's license.

"Don't you drive at home?"

"I lost my license."

"How?"

"They said I was drunk." She turned her head slightly and gave me a corner-of-the-eye look. She seemed to be inviting my incredulity. What she earned was my silent disapproval. So I was not wrong to find her drinking ominously excessive.

"Drive as seldom as you can," I advised her. "It's always wiser to walk in Rome."

"Don't worry about your car."

"I'm worried about you."

This touched her. Her eyes became moist, and she leaned toward me from the driver's seat. I kissed her chastely and said good-by.

"Hurry back."

"I'll let you know."

When I stood on the sidewalk with my bags around me and watched her direct the Fiat into traffic, my final words sounded like a promise to warn her before I reappeared in Rome.

From the Stazione Termini, I took the airport bus for 1500 lire. It was a bumpy, uncomfortable ride but, once we got out of town and were in the country, the scenery was beautiful, particularly the cypresses on the horizon, which looked deliberately shaped. When one drives in Italy, the last thing he is able to enjoy is the sights.

Having checked my bags through passport control, I went into the duty-free shop and bought a carton of Marlboros. The package of cigarettes I had bought in Fiumicino the afternoon before had been left behind in my apartment. Not deliberately. I had simply forgotten them, and the perverse desire to smoke a cigarette was suddenly strong in me again. The thought of someone my own age dead made caution for my health seem ludicrous. Walking down the long rubber-matted corridor to my gate, I was reminded of my departure from Washington years ago, when a randomly purchased magazine had turned me into a writer of stories for boys. A run up to New York to see my agent would enable me to write off this trip as a business expense.

I asked for and got a seat at the very back of the rear cabin of the 747. As the huge body tapers the rows of seats grow shorter, until you arrive at a couple of rows of two seats each. The one beside mine was unoccupied. Perfect. It is impossible to get completely out of range of the movie, but one can read and sleep and drink in relative peace there in the rear of the plane.

I carried aboard my typewriter and a bag bulging with newspapers and my current reading, a life of Conrad that had taken a hundred thousand words to get the man out of Poland. I would have been better advised to read the life of Max Brand, Rex Stout or Erle Stanley Gardner, fellow hacks, but I persisted in the outrageous assumption that, despite the looks of my oeuvre—my ninety-third novel was about to appear—I was destined to rub shoulders with the likes of Conrad. Existing as I did pseudonymously, on the fringes of the literary world, I was unlikely, before or after shuffling off this mortal coil, to receive the attention Connolly was getting.

The *Rome Daily American* and the *Corriere della Sera* contained lengthy hagiographic accounts. *Il Giornale* had a somewhat confusing piece written by an Italian whose conception of the United States had apparently been gleaned from the novels of Louis L'Amour. *Der Zeit* hinted broadly at the possibility of Vatican machinations, and the reader was not discouraged from thinking that an agent for the Curia had planted a bomb aboard the fateful

1 8

plane. Connolly was seen as an intrepid original theologian, willing to take risks, considering no dogma immune to skeptical reevaluation. It was an odd conception of the theologian's task, but it had certainly been Connolly's own.

Several weak Manhattans helped to wash down my reading. The lights of the cabin were dimmed for the movie, but I read on in the glow of the lamp above my seat. The biography of Conrad put me to sleep. Unconscious at thirty thousand feet, my head ahum with dreams, I was borne back to my native land, to my no-longer wife and to Connolly's obsequies, an unknown author coming home.

Chapter 4

Cardinals were there, the apostolic delegate was there, veterans of various domestic wars and protests of the past fifteen years were there—e.g., both the Berrigans and quorums of the Norfolk Six and Pasadena Twelve. Needless to say, theologians were there in abundance, those such by benefit of degree as well as those guilty only by long association with the former. There were nuns, of course, no longer recognizable by wimple and veil, but unmistakably nunnish nonetheless, no matter the raising of consciousness and skirt. The place was packed.

The place in question was the National Shrine of the Immaculate Conception on the campus of the Catholic University of America in Washington, D.C., a building that may be described as a cross between Sacré Coeur and the hangar Howard Hughes built to house the Spruce Goose. The height of the nave is such that there would be time for a parachute to open should anyone equipped with a parachute plummet from its highest point. From the back of the church, the sanctuary appears to be in the next county. It is a mystery that an edifice of such dimensions fails to impress as does, say, the Cathedral of Cologne. If I had been in charge of Connolly's funeral, I would have insisted on St. Matthew's downtown or even, in these ecumenical days, the National Cathedral. Better a tasteful replica than a mystifying original. And of course the media were there. They swarmed—still photographers, others with television cameras strapped to their shoulders like orthopedic devices, columnists, commentators. The only medium missing was the kind that gets in touch with the departed.

I could imagine the solemn commentaries being whispered into all those tape recorders. The funeral was not being covered live, not because of the logical difficulties a live funeral suggests, but because Connolly was not a Kennedy. Yet I would wager that the politicians in the front pews (among them the Vice-President, there in a dual capacity, representing both the administration and himself as an alumnus of Newman Hall—little Francis Conway come a long way from the shores of Lake Jemima) would not draw a crowd like Connolly's when they died. Among the churchmen in the sanctuary, only Father Hesburgh was likely to get a send-off like this.

Connolly had not had a parachute when he plummeted from a height considerably greater than that of the National Shrine, he and fifty-odd other passengers the victims of a private plane's wandering into their path as the flight from Chicago descended along the Potomac. Pictures of police and the National Guard gathering fragments of bodies had livened TV screens and front pages, prompting the usual demands that the FAA impose more stringent regulations on commercial carriers and private aircraft. Necessarily, it was a closed-coffin affair, such fractions of Connolly as were being sent on their way by the Mass of the Angels unsuitable for viewing. With the kind of coverage the accident received, it can scarcely be considered ghoulish to imagine the cabin of the 727 during its final moments.

Returning from a lecture tour that had drawn an unusual amount of publicity even for him, Connolly could be forgiven if he felt proud but pooped. His topic had been John Paul II's Holy Thursday letter on the Eucharist, not the sort of thing you might have thought would engage Connolly's debating skills, but that had always been part of his appeal, the incommensurability between the cause of his dissent and its flamboyance. The pope had asked priests to renew the promises and commitments undertaken at the time of their ordination, and Connolly drew out the insidious implications of the papal letter.

It said a lot about the American episcopacy that the Cardinal Archbishop of Washington should be presiding at the obsequies of a man who had given him and his predecessors conniptions for a decade and a half. When the ecclesiastical procession passed our pew, Nancy whispered, "They're here to make sure he's dead."

Nancy, my companion in our now null and void marriage, had sounded unsurprised when I telephoned her from Dulles. "You heard about Michael?" she asked.

"You're kidding."

Her pause was meant to chide me, I suppose. Kidding on an occasion as solemn as this? Heloise should have it so good. "Where are you?"

"Dulles."

"Where are you staying?"

"I haven't made arrangements."

"That's dumb. This is Washington in the spring. Look, take a cab here and in the meantime I'll try to find a hotel for you."

"Here" was her apartment off Colfax Circle, where, rumor in the form of our old classmate Nose Bauer had it, the Reverend Michael Connolly had been a frequent overnight guest. It seemed fitting that the news came as it did, via a chartered flight for pilgrims. See the Holy Land with Father Bauer. Thus ran the ads in the diocesan paper, a beaming picture of Nose, a breathless list of the edifying places to be seen under his expert tutelage, the cost, and a coupon to be filled out and mailed as soon as possible, this is a limited offer. Thaddeus Bauer, pastor of St. Thomas More parish in White Rapids, Wisconsin, was wonderfully untouched by all that had happened in the Church since his ordination.

"I thought you knew, Jim. I didn't mean to come bearing scandal."

"She's not my wife, Ted." I could not call him Nose to his face, not after all these years. "She obtained an annulment."

Bauer sat on the edge of his chair, knees apart to accommodate his belly and the hands that dangled between them, one holding a glass of Campari. He shook his head. "Annulments! We've become a laughingstock. Marriage courts have become what Reno used to be. It makes all the fuss over Henry VIII look ridiculous. My parish is St. Thomas More."

"I heard."

This pleased him. "I suppose everyone who comes to Rome looks you up."

"Some."

"I got your address from Harry."

"He's been here."

But Harry had telephoned before showing up on my doorstep, giving me a chance to get Maria out of the apartment. A banging on my door brought me from my typewriter to find Bauer standing there, a camera slung around his neck, his clothes rumpled, a gap-toothed smile radiating across the years since I had last seen him. He began to pound my upper arms.

"*Ciao*, you old bandit. *Buon giorno* and how the hell are you?" He stepped back, to get perspective on me. "A little less thatch on the roof, Jim, but I'd know you in a crowd. Show me your pad."

He showed himself around, but if he noticed any clue to Maria's living there he said not a thing. I did not want her showing up while he was still there. She had wandered out, vaguely intent on doing a little shopping. A little shopping. With Maria, acquiring new things, particularly clothes, was a neurosis. With any luck she would not be back before noon, which gave me not quite two hours in which to be hospitable to Bauer and then send him on his way. I offered him a drink and, it being before noon, he closed an eye and cocked his head.

"Really going down the chute, huh?"

I poured him a Campari, which he sniffed and tasted and likened to mouthwash. He actually gargled a little to underline the point. And then we settled down to the inevitable roll call of old classmates: Harry Wilson, Himer, Shaw, Hirschberger, Farrell, the whole bunch. The Vice-President and Connolly were the big ones, of course, so not much time passed before Bauer expressed his disgust that Connolly was shacking up with Nancy.

"Annulment or not, it's a rotten thing to do to an old friend, forget about morality."

I could not agree more. On the other hand, sympathy was not something I wanted from Nose Bauer. My apparent indifference to the scandalous duo bothered him a bit.

Did he expect me to start throwing furniture around? Among other things, I did not want to strike a moral stance that would be made ridiculous if Maria walked in the door.

What Bauer said really did not surprise me. It was the verification of the gloomy thoughts I had whenever, weary of the life I was leading, I recalled the four years of our marriage, Adam nostalgic for Eden. I did doubt it was as flagrant as Bauer suggested. Such stories acquire a hyperbolic cast in the mouths of tellers true to the vocation to which they have been called. Nancy's move to take a job with the National Bishops Conference in Washington, where Connolly retained precarious tenure at the Catholic University, had obvious implications. Perhaps Connolly had even helped her get the job. Given the Trojan horse nature of the staff there, it was possible he would have influence.

When I got out of the cab in front of her building, the air was scented, bird song was audible, April was being the cruelest month again. Nancy's voice over the intercom sounded metallic, but when I emerged from the elevator and saw her waiting in her open doorway I thought, just so she must have greeted Connolly. She was aging well. There was no trace of the saucy coed type who had painted watercolors on the balcony of our hotel room in Rome. Perhaps hers was the dignity of the ersatz widow.

"You look good," I said.

"You've put on weight."

"Well, my hair is thinner."

"I noticed. Is that the reason for the beard?"

"Welcome to Washington," I said, but I was not really annoyed. Nancy took from me the bag stuffed with newspapers I had bought in Rome.

"Oh, good. I want to see those."

She wore a navy blue linen dress with white piping, and

white heels, the dress nipped in at the waist by a white cincture. Her hair was cut short in a sensible way, and the few strands of gray blended easily into its ashen blondness. When I was inside and she had shut the door, she turned to me, avoiding my eye. Maybe she felt as I had with Nose Bauer in my apartment, wondering if I would detect the absent one.

"All the hotels are full," she said, dropping the newspapers in a corner of the couch.

"How biblical."

"You can stay here, if you like." She looked at me then, eyes cold, daring me to say the wrong thing. "There's an extra room."

I managed only to nod. Annulments, like divorces, confer on the woman one has slept with the status of untouchable, increasing her attractiveness. The thought of staying with Nancy was welcome in an illicit way, and repellent.

Looking past her at the bookshelves in a corner of the room, I saw the row of Connolly's books, but I also saw a small photograph in a silver frame. Gregory. I was tired from the flight and affected by Nancy's cool attractiveness, and the sight of that picture of our dead son brought me dangerously close to tears. Dear God, what we had been through together, Nancy and I. Even if it had meant the end of us as well as of our son, there had been months when we were more united in grief than we ever were by love. No civil or church court could render that null and void. I had snapshots of my son, one in my wallet, but I was completely disarmed by Gregory's picture on a shelf in his mother's apartment.

After Greg's death, it became one of my conceits that I was more affected by what had happened than Nancy. The German blood from her mother's side enabled her to get through the awfulness without breaking down. Within a month she removed all his toys and clothes, firm in the conviction that we must not indulge ourselves in wasting sorrow. That is not the Irish way. I concealed under the handkerchiefs in my drawer a little rubber duck Greg loved to have in the bath with him. When squeezed it squeaked, and in the tub squeezing filled it with water, and I had played the stream about to Greg's delight, stirring precocious interest in arcing, perhaps. One day I found the duck was gone. Nancy was in the room and saw me searching around among my socks and underwear.

"I threw it out, Jim."

She gave me an even look as she said this, the very expression with which she followed the little coffin down the aisle after the funeral—unlike Niobe, no tears. Walking beside her then, unable not to cry, I put a hand to my trembling mouth and Nancy's arm tightened in mine, to give me strength, I suppose. The sight of her, stoic, chin up, filled me with momentary hatred. Yet after the funeral, when we were alone, she came into my arms and wept uncontrollably.

But that, it seemed, was that. She erased all memories of Greg from our home. I should have known she would find the duck and see in it a symbol of my Celtic need for keening. There must have been hatred in my eyes when she told me what she had done. She awaited an outburst from me, but I did not accommodate her. A few pictures and his baby book were our only proof we had had a son.

Three months after he died, Greg's birthday came around. He would have been two years old. As the date approached, I waited for Nancy to say something. Surely that reminder of our loss would get to her. I felt she needed to grieve, to weep.

What would have been Greg's second birthday fell on a Saturday. I had decided to go to Mass—to invoke his prayers, not pray for him; what harm had he done in the

2 7

short span of his life? And I was determined to go alone. I became convinced that Nancy had put him so thoroughly out of her mind she wouldn't remember what day it was anyway. I was ready to lie when I came into the kitchen at 7:30 to find a note. "Gone to get milk. N." Good. I didn't need the car to get to church.

It was the first Saturday of the month, and the devotion prompted by the Blessed Virgin's apparitions at Fatima made for an untypically full church that morning. I almost resented the intrusion of all those people into my private commemoration. Father Bacci, the pastor, was at the altar, wearing an old bass fiddle kind of chasuble, his back to the congregation. Bacci disapproved of *Alleluia*, which he saw, not without reason, as subversive of the Church as he knew it. Nancy and I had sat through more than one sermon that was a point by point refutation of some piece in the magazine. He was already reading the epistle lickety-split when I came in. I went up a side aisle, past the confessionals and banks of vigil lights, and slipped into a pew. Only a few minutes passed before I noticed Nancy a few rows ahead of me wearing the scarf she had bought in Puerto Rico on our belated honeymoon.

Nancy had already made the five first Saturdays. That was not why she was here. There was no possible doubt as to what had brought her to Mass that morning. There were several things I might have done, should have done. Most obvious, I could have knelt beside her. I could have stayed where I was and waited for her afterward. This was something to bring us close again. There was no need for words. What I did do was leave the church. I was mad as hell, as if Nancy had ruined the occasion for me, spoiled my chance to whip myself into a frenzy of grief. But if I was intent on mourning our son in private, so too was Nancy. She had not wanted me at her side.

Neither of us ever mentioned it, but of course, of the

two of us, I was the only one who knew. I was drinking coffee and reading the paper when Nancy returned and plunked down a carton of milk. Her secret was mine and I could not bear to look at her.

So too, come from Europe, I did not allude to the framed picture of Greg on the bookshelf in her living room.

Ensconced in the extra bedroom, showered, shaved and restored to respectability, I pushed away thoughts of those days when Nancy and I were tackling dummies on the practice field of life.

"Do I smell a cigarette?" Nancy looked in at me with a surprised smile.

"Doctor's orders."

"Which doctor?"

"That's the one. A really gruesome mask. Where is the funeral?"

She told me. "He'll be waked tonight. I don't plan to go."

"I'm with you."

"He'll be buried in Wisconsin. On the grounds of your old school."

"Who decided that?"

"Michael?"

As students there, Connolly and I had imagined returning to the faculty of Newman Hall when we were priests. That was not an ambition compatible with the parish work we seemed more likely to be engaged in, and when, during vacations, I saw the life the pastor and assistant of my home parish led, I realized it was not for me. It was a good thing. Theories against such preparatory seminaries as Newman Hall were developed, and eventually the lakeshore property and buildings were sold. An evangelical sect now occupied the site of my boyhood memories.

At the time of the sale, Connolly was spending a postdoctoral summer teaching at Notre Dame. On assignment for *Alleluia* to visit Friendship House in Chicago, I drove east on U.S. 20 to South Bend. With a nice view of the Golden Dome, in the shadow of Father Sorin's statue, Connolly and I sat on a bench and talked.

"Where will you be in the fall?" I asked him.

He plucked a clover from the lawn beside the bench and denuded it of leaves. It did not have four. "Do you know the Carmelite convent near Black River Falls?"

"You're taking the veil?"

He tossed aside the stem of the clover. "Brady wants me to be chaplain there. I've been advised to turn my dissertation into a book. I'll have all the time in the world there. I got an offer from Catholic University, but Brady says I have to finish the book first."

"And then he'll let you go?"

Connolly shrugged. He and his bishop were not yet adversaries. "My sister is a member of that community."

Catherine. A year Connolly's junior, she might have been a distracting presence on visiting Sunday at Newman Hall if it were not for her unnerving otherworldly eyes. Like Connolly she was tall, but unlike him she accepted it and had a regal carriage. An interest in Edith Stein played a part in her own vocation to Carmel.

Connolly held that chaplaincy for two years, and he did write his book, a dangerously original one on theological language. Brady was not pleased, but he kept his promise about Catholic University. Perhaps he thought he was getting rid of a troublesome priest. The book was savaged in several reviews, and it was to offset their impact that I did an article on it for *Alleluia*. That paean of praise for Connolly was the first thing of mine that Nancy read.

"Give me one of those," Nancy said after she had fed me, indicating my box of Marlboros. We were in the

3 0

living room, my back to the photograph of Greg, staring across the years to what had become of his parents.

"They smell better than they taste," Nancy said, after I had given her a cigarette and lit it for her.

"How long has it been?"

"I quit when everyone did. When did you go back to them?"

"Yesterday."

She thought about that but said nothing, doubtless making the connection with the news of Connolly's death. He was very much with us then, moving wraithlike with the cigarette smoke that swirled in ghostly arabesques in the room. I asked when she had last seen Connolly.

"Just before he left on his lecture tour." She had not hesitated. "We spoke of you."

"Do you have anything to drink?"

She got up. "I suppose we should have an Irish wake."

She left her cigarette smoldering in a pewter ashtray that looked vaguely familiar. Apparently she had not got rid of all traces of our life together. Several things in the room dated from our marriage—a lamp, a table, the couch I sat on. There had been no signs of Connolly in the bedroom Nancy had given me. I checked her bedroom too, leaving the water running in the bathroom to conceal my movements. The razor in the medicine cabinet could have been Nancy's own. There was no shaving cream, but he would have taken that with him. I sidled into Nancy's room and looked around.

A small lamp with a pink ribbed shade was on beside the bed. In its glow the expanse of the bed elicited sweet painful memories. There was a perfumed smell in the room. The closet door was ajar and there hung Nancy's dresses, all in a row, arranged seasonally. Stages on life's way. The jewelry box on the dresser was flanked by jars and bottles, tubes and atomizers. It was a room where I did not belong, though there were no signs of any other male occupant. I backed into the hall, my shoulder blades atingle, but my invasion was unobserved. I began to hope that Bauer's story was only slander.

The apartment reminded me of Nancy's place in the Village when she came to work for *Alleluia*, fresh from the convent. It was a time when leaving seemed a more serious decision than staying. John XXIII had called for open windows, and through them had exited thousands of nuns and priests, trailing the dreams of their youth. Nancy retained the zeal and altruism that had made a religious vocation tempting, and she was eager to find out what it meant to be a Catholic in the 1960s. She did copyediting and was responsible for assigning books to reviewers. Gilligan liked her. Everybody liked her. I loved her. Neither of us could have known what lay ahead for us.

We married, moved to Queens, Gregory was born, fell ill and died, and we were faced with the task of redefining our lives. When Connolly turned down the offer to represent *Alleluia* at the Council and Gilligan turned to me, it seemed exactly what we needed. Here was a chance to escape the scene of our sadness. Nancy had come back to *Alleluia* after Greg's death, but her heart was no longer in it. The thought of going to Rome made her seem once more the girl I had married.

"What about your art lessons?" I asked.

"I can paint anywhere."

By unspoken agreement we did not want another child. It would have seemed disloyal, as if we were seeking a replacement for Greg. I had come upon the cardboard wheel of pills containing Nancy's daily dose of infertility and said nothing. My reticence had nothing to do with the wrangling of moral theologians. Nancy's art classes were at once therapy and a search for a creativity other than motherhood. She urged me to complete the novel I had begun in Vietnam.

I had lasted through the first two years of the major seminary before I left to join the Marine Corps. Eight weeks of the horror of boot camp were rewarded with a leave. With my hair grown to almost respectable length again, I went to visit my old classmates. There was the expected hooting at the sight of me in dress blues, but Connolly studied me with approval.

"Don't get your ass shot off," he advised.

"More or less my own sentiments."

"Where do you go now?"

I knew but saw no reason to burden him with it. Vietnam awaited me after further training at Camp Pendleton in California. If I did not make more of it this might have been due to the memory of how odd Korean veterans had seemed to us, men of twenty and more who did not know Latin. Rather than a potential hero, I felt like one of those late bloomers who had been the objects of our mirth.

I did not get my ass shot off. In Pendleton the chaplain took me under his wing, and I spent my war as an altar boy, carting around his Mass kit in the steaming jungle. You have seen the photographs: craggy-faced priest lifts chalice heavenward to the deity who is fortunately on our side, chasuble whipped by the breeze, gun-toting grunts on one knee, hollow-eyed, unshaven, devout beneath their rough exteriors. Not a typical scene for Captain Hardy and myself, however. For the most part we stayed in the relative security of a huge naval base north of Saigon with first-run movies, good chow, lots of visiting politicians and a slop chute that featured Coors beer. I read *The Quiet American* on location—there was a good library on the base—and spent a lot of time trading seminary stories with Hardy.

33

The letters Connolly sent me in Vietnam were full of theologians I had never heard of: Rahner, von Balthasar, Lonergan. I was trying to write. At my desk in the chaplain's office I picked away at a Selectric, working on a novel inspired by Graham Greene, an idea he had discarded. It concerned the last pope, maintained as a curiosity by the godless regime, wandering the world in search of remnants of faith and finding none. The pope and the dictator who spared him as a joke grow old, and finally the dictator decides to rid the world of this last relic of religious belief. He will execute the pope himself. He does, and in the moment after he fires the shot he wonders, "What if that old man's beliefs were true?" A new Christian is born in sorrow.

I could not believe my luck that Greene had left the idea in the public domain. Photocopies of finished chapters went off to Connolly in Wisconsin for praise and criticism. My attempt at fiction must have seemed frivolous to him, immersed as he was in theology. That was the novel Nancy urged me to finish. I tried and I could not bring it off, but my efforts proved to be the apprenticeship of a juvenile novelist.

Nancy's other great concern at the time was Evelyn, the receptionist at *Alleluia*, who became pregnant. The putative father was the priest who had received Evelyn into the Church. Spiritual counseling had led to intimacy, but by the time Evelyn realized her condition her mentor had left his parish and decamped to San Francisco and a debauch among the flower children.

"He has to be told," Nancy said to me.

"Maybe he already knows. It could be why he left."

"Evelyn doesn't think so."

"Her judgments are not reliable."

"Jim!"

I deserved her disapproval and, as penance, suffered the

weeping presence of Evelyn in our house. She was from Iowa, and among the issues discussed was whether her parents should be told. But the real problem was should she bear the child or not.

"The decision is yours," Nancy would tell her.

"What would I do if I had it?"

"Put the baby up for adoption."

Nancy favored this, but she did not press it on Evelyn. I listened with foreboding. Would Nancy offer to adopt Evelyn's child? That was a proposal I dreaded. I did not want the bastard child of a priest and a naive girl from Iowa taking the place left vacant by Greg. In bed at night, Evelyn asleep on the couch in our living room, I lay sleepless beside Nancy, fearing what compassion might drive her to.

"I could wring his neck," she said of Bailey, the flown father. I imagined him, long-haired and bearded, wandering the streets of Haight-Ashbury in a poncho.

"It takes two to tango."

"He took advantage of her. The funny thing is that this hasn't shaken her faith."

I thought of Evelyn, with her weak eyes, narrow face and lank hair, and failed to find a suggestion of spiritual depth. What could not be denied was the child forming in her womb. Soon she would have to stay away from the offices of *Alleluia*.

"Maybe she should get an abortion," I said.

"She thinks it's wrong."

"So do I. But there are many wrongs. Like being twenty-three and an unmarried mother in Manhattan."

"I think she should have the baby."

"She'll never see it again if she puts it up for adoption. All she'll have is the pain."

Silence from Nancy. I felt I could hear her suggestion that we take the baby. I turned on my side and feigned

35

sleep. Nancy and I lived almost like brother and sister now. Sex is the instrument of hope and, since Greg's death, we had tasted despair. But there was a deeper absence than sex in my life. Nancy fell asleep. I tried to imagine a God presiding over our days and could not. Memories of faith came easily, but they were memories, having nothing to do with the present. My lack of faith became a secret more desperate than Evelyn's.

Evelyn disappeared and there were days of anguish. Should we notify the police? Finally we did, and Evelyn was located in the hospital where she had rid herself of the consequence of her folly. Nancy went to visit her. Once. I think she felt betrayed. A month later Gilligan asked me to go to Rome.

Nancy returned with Scotch and ice and glasses and asked me to make the drinks. Scotch on the rocks. Connolly's drink. I thought of him lolling on my couch after the first session with his inquisitors in Rome. The realization that he was dead came to me then.

"It's hard to believe." I immediately regretted the trite remark.

"You told me once he had a premonition he would die young."

"Did I? I don't remember."

"I do." She made it sound as if I wanted him dead. Did I? What difference did it make now? My Michael Connolly was a figure of memory rather than the well-publicized dissident who had gone up and down in the world reinterpreting the Creed.

"I wonder if he realized he'd lost his faith."

"He still had it, in his sense of the term."

"How about you?" I asked.

"What do you mean?"

"Do you still go to Mass, confess your sins, pray?"

"Don't you?"

"No."

In the silence we sipped our drinks, and I was very conscious of the photograph behind me, as if Gregory had heard my awful admission. Yes, awful. I had not discarded the outlook of a lifetime easily. My faith had faded away and disappeared, and one day I realized it was gone. And grieved over the loss. With Connolly I might pretend it was an achievement, a matter of simple honesty, but to lose the faith is to be a loser indeed. Losing was something I seemed good at. After all, I had also lost Greg and Nancy.

"Tell me about your job, Nancy."

She spoke with enthusiasm and in detail, but what came through was her sense of doing something worthwhile and important. Her title was executive director. Her passion was Central America and the mistakes the Church had made there. I stirred uneasily, a writer of books for boys, one of which had been set in a Yucatán I had never seen.

"I'm fed up with theoretical squabbles," she said. "We have to make the world a better place."

"That makes Connolly seem trivial."

"Didn't you hear his speech on Nicaragua?"

Nicaragua? It was hard enough to take Connolly seriously on the Creed. On foreign policy he would know as much as I had of Yucatán.

"It all hangs together, Jim." Nancy took another cigarette from the box I had left on the coffee table. "Michael planned to meet with Segundo."

What would have become of us if Gregory had lived? Nancy spoke with authority about the Third World, and I churned out novels for kids. Her enthusiasm linked her to Connolly, not to me, nor was that an accident. We had never discussed the incident that had prompted my abrupt departure from Rome.

"Will you go to Mass tomorrow?" she asked.

"That's why I came."

"But not to communion?"

"No."

She let it go. We had another Scotch on the rocks together, and I had another after she had gone to bed. To return for Connolly's funeral seemed a posthumous collusion in his betrayal of me.

As the time of communion approached the following day, in the National Shrine, I thought, now I will learn if Nancy is still a communicant, but I was distracted by images of her seated at Greg's bedside in the hospital and comforting the weeping Evelyn. Her compassion convicted me of triviality. The homily had been preached by Hughes, current president of the American Catholic Theological Society, once of Fordham, now of Yale, and it was a eulogy of hyperbolic excess, putting Michael Connolly right up there with Augustine, Anselm, Aquinas and Calvin. Yes, Calvin. I looked for wincing among the prelates on the altar but they retained expressions of preoccupied solemnity. Oh, for a modern Dante who would not blanch at distributing his contemporaries in purgatory if not hell as well as heaven. If these locations are taken to be mystical, I suppose it does not matter if everyone is herded through the pearly gates.

Nancy received communion. Ninety-five percent of those in the huge church, Protestants as well as Catholics, went forward to receive under both species. Not even thoughts of my first communion at the age of eight could make me envy them. What had become of that little boy with slicked-down hair, all in white, even a white prayerbook clamped between joined hands as he frowned against the sunlight when my mother took the picture? In the years that followed, receiving the body and blood of Christ had become routine. Nancy returned with bowed head to kneel beside me and commune with her Lord. Was she remembering Gregory then?

The organ boomed, the casket was rolled down the aisle, followed by the lengthy procession of clerics. Since burial was to be in Wisconsin, there was a lot of milling around on the steps outside, and then Gilligan came through the crowd to Nancy and me.

"There's going to be some kind of reception across the street at the Oblate house. Why don't you come?"

Gilligan had grown fat and veins were visible on his flaming cheeks. The style of his glasses was new but this pair, like all the others, slid down his nose, necessitating a constant upward push with the middle finger of his hand. In the offices of *Alleluia* we had an obscene description of that gesture which would have shocked Gilligan. At seventy he had seen much, but he remained a kind of Catholic one does not meet often anymore. It was like him not to show surprise at seeing Nancy and me together.

"Let's," Nancy said to me, having given Gilligan a kiss. This embarrassed the old man, and he got out his pipe and put it between his dentures.

Flanking Gilligan, we started for the corner, where we could cross Massachusetts Avenue. There was a flow in that direction. Gilligan did not know who had arranged the reception.

"Jude Dougherty told me about it."

Dougherty, dean of the School of Philosophy at Catholic University, had been an outspoken critic of Connolly. I wondered what sort of group we were joining. All I asked was a drink.

The crème de la crème were there, notables of the sixties and seventies, Connolly's rivals for public attention: intellectuals, activists, two nuns I did not recognize—one tall, one short, both wearing round white pins on which was lettered in blue ORDAIN WOMEN. The tall one glared at me; I could not think why, unless she remembered a spoof I had written years before about a man who wanted to become a nun. Humor is not rife among ideologues. Ordain women, indeed.

Dan Berrigan wore a multicolored sweater, jeans and suede ankle-high shoes. His graying hair was combed forward, and the sad, long-suffering expression in his eyes marked him as the poet he essentially was. When Nancy and I joined him, he was telling a tall, bald man with unblinking eyes and a knifelike nose of his last visit to Gethsemani to see Tom Merton.

"In the hermitage?" The man's nod invited an affirmative answer.

He got it, and then Dan noticed Nancy, took her hand and stooped to kiss her cheek. The medallion he wore around his neck swung free. Nancy mentioned the funeral Mass.

"A gathering of eagles," he said wryly.

"Is that why you didn't concelebrate?"

He crinkled his eyes enigmatically and asked me what I was doing now.

"I'm living in Rome."

His eyes widened, but I did not explain. Imagine telling Dan Berrigan I was now a prolific author of books for children. I asked if he still wrote poetry.

"Not much."

His name was called and he turned away. Gilligan, who had been separated from us in the crush, reappeared with a drink in his hand. I asked where he had got it, and Nancy and I followed him to the bar where we picked up Bloody Marys. Mike Novak came up and asked Gilligan about *Alleluia*. Circulation continued to drop, Gilligan said glumly. Issues of the magazine grew ever slimmer.

"Isn't it curious," Novak said in his high voice, "that all this renewal is killing off Catholic journalism?"

"Not the *National Catholic Reporter*," Nancy said.

A column seemed to form behind Novak's narrow eyes but he smiled fulsomely at Nancy. "*Columbia* is flourishing too." This was the magazine of the Knights of Columbus.

Gilligan dipped into his drink and said wet-lipped to me, "You should come back and liven us up."

"Do you need a Rome correspondent?"

"I can't afford it."

"I'm cheap."

"Are you serious?"

"No."

Gilligan looked relieved. The tall nun with the button on her bosom suddenly confronted me.

"You are James Clark," she said.

I put out my hand and she deliberately ignored it. Her eyes were alight with righteousness, and she was clearly looking for an argument.

"You're mistaking me for my brother, the writer."

"Your brother?"

"He was on the staff of *Alleluia*. Do you know the editor, Mr. Gilligan?"

Gilligan bowed, ignoring her button. He probably favored women priests in the secret conviction it would never happen.

"I'm a subscriber," the nun said. Her smile exposed as much gums as teeth. I edged away.

"Coward," Nancy whispered.

We worked the crowd together: Charlie Curran, Avery Dulles, Germain Grisez, Gus Wallace the Dominican, probably there only because he lived across the street. Garry Wills, pudgy and frowning, looked curiously around, not listening to what Jim Hitchcock was saying to him. By now the bar had become common knowledge, and it would have been impossible to get another drink. Gregory Baum and Malachi Martin were chin to chin, and I suggested to Nancy that we go outside. The party had spilled onto the lawn.

Nancy said, "What do you do in Rome?"

"Not much."

"I mean, how do you earn a living?"

I had expected this question last night, and I was ready for it. "I represent an American firm."

"What kind of firm?"

"They publish."

"You're a salesman?"

I laughed. "Not quite. I put packages together."

"What's the name of the firm?"

"Badger Inc." This was true. My accountant, Putzer, who had been recommended by my literary agent, Cassell, suggested for tax purposes that I incorporate, so I did. The copyright to all my books was in the name of Badger Inc.

"It sounds very mysterious."

"Well, it enables me to live in Rome, and that's the important thing."

"Rome," Nancy murmured. "How I hated it there."

Hated it? I was genuinely surprised. We had not had much money there, but Rome was cheap. I had thought Nancy enjoyed painting. I had thought she liked it. Or did she have other things in mind when she said she hated Rome? I certainly did not want to pursue that.

"Do you still paint?"

"No!"

"I thought you were pretty good."

She searched my face for irony. The sunlight was kept from her face by her hat, and her wide eyes reminded me of how much I had loved her. "I'm not creative in that way."

"You should take it up again." From where we stood I looked kitty-corner across the intersection at the huge dome of the Shrine and the bluer sky beyond.

"Sunday painters are a bore."

"Then paint on weekdays."

"I don't have time. Jim, let's get out of here."

"Where's a nice place I can take you to lunch?"

There was a Greek place in Georgetown she had heard good things about.

"Let's find out."

How uxorious I felt with her when I was not remembering her treachery with Connolly, the sonofabitch. I repeated it to myself. The sonofabitch. After the excesses of the homily, it felt good to get his classification right.

The restaurant was unassumingly nice, its menu free of the varieties of quiche that seemed to have swept the country. We ordered shish kebab and ouzo. Nancy in her polka dot dress and white picture hat was a striking presence across the table from me, and it was pleasant to notice the glances she drew from the other diners. The faintly absurd feeling I had appearing in public with Maria was suddenly clear by contrast. A woman in her forties can be more attractive than one in her twenties. Life had written some lines on Nancy's soul even if they had not yet appeared on her face. And I was relieved of the need to amuse. There was little danger Nancy would fall into a sulk if the world stopped titillating her for a moment.

"You must go to Wisconsin for the burial, Jim."

"Are you going?"

"I can't. You were his oldest friend, Jim. He admired you a lot."

I could imagine them speaking of me. Poor Jim, so brilliant, why is he vegetating in Rome? Connolly had never asked me how I earned my bread.

"I suppose I should. I have to go to New York too."

I had cabled Cassell that I would be in the States and hoped to see him.

"What for?"

"I haven't been there in ages."

Chapter 5

Parked in a rented car, I looked across Lake Jemima at the squat tile-roofed tower of what had once been Newman Hall and was now Bethel Evangelical Center. No doubt it was fitting that it be renamed by its new owners, its infant baptism considered invalid. I needed distance from the place, the intermediary of the lake, to restore those buildings to the familiar coordinates of memory.

From where I sat, the island did not seem an island, but blended into the far shore. On its high point stood the little chapel dedicated to the Virgin Mary, gift of a benefactress of Newman Hall who now lay buried beneath the granite floor of her gift. An hour before, Michael Connolly had been lowered into a grave in the shadow of the chapel.

I had wandered through the school with a pained proprietary air, past the empty niche that had contained a statue of the boy Jesus, down a now-carpeted corridor from whose vaulted ceiling a series of chandeliers descended like an arrested stick of bombs. The former study hall was now a warren of business offices, the auditorium had been turned into radio and television studios whose programs reached out through ether and brought back customers for the correspondence Bible courses, the records, tapes, books and pamphlets. But it remained a school too, and the corridor was filled with young people with fresh innocent faces who looked me in the eye with the assurance of the saved. They were good as gold, I was certain of it. Surely worse things could have happened to this place. But what did these refreshing fundamentalists make of the Latin inscriptions chipped into the walls, the Catholic symbols twisted into the flung-back wrought-iron gates flanking the chapel entrance? The chapel was the greatest shock.

The oak pews were the same, though they had been painted white, but absent from the sanctuary was the altar with its great ivory phoenix on a field of gold and, bordering its canopy, the Vulgate verse I had, from my place in the front pew, laboriously translated during my second semester of Latin. The sanctuary now contained an organ and, as centerpiece, a pulpit as white as the pews. The stations of the cross were still embedded in marble along the side aisles, and on either side of the door the holy water stoups remained. What did these Roman artifacts mean to the current occupants? Thus it must have been in the early days of the Reformation when churches had been converted to a new observance.

The ceremony took place in the chapel, and the audience was one half Bible students and one half mourners for Michael Connolly, his fellow priests for the most part.

4 6

Bishop Lowry stood at the edge of the sanctuary wearing cope and miter and read apologetically from the book his master of ceremonies held before him. The priests in the pews wore street dress. I recognized only two of them; the rest were younger than Connolly and myself. He would have been their hero as he had not been for his peers. With exceptions, of course.

Lowry began the brief ceremony by thanking the current owners for the use of the chapel and for permitting Connolly to be buried on the grounds as he had requested. How had the request been made? Lowry did not say. Had Connolly been misunderstood when he said Newman Hall would be sold over his dead body? My facetiousness was self-protective. How could I not be overwhelmed by memories in that chapel? I was the last one in the world to mock Connolly's wish to be buried there. Maybe I should ask the Reverend Baker if he would mind my ashes' being scattered over the lake from a hired plane when my own time came. Ash Wednesday. Oh, the Lents that had begun there, I on my knees promising impossible things. I would keep the rule to the letter, I would stop smoking, give up desserts, be friendly with people I did not like, pray.

The coffin in the center aisle invited similar resolutions now, as if simply by being in that chapel I had regained the faith of my youth. But my heart, like the sanctuary, had been stripped of its tabernacle, leaving only the words of men. Lowry read quickly, as if he were doing something disreputable in the wrong place. And then it was over. I remained where I was, trusting to my beard and the intervening years to render me unrecognizable. The procession went out, the handful of priests contrasting with the pomp of the Washington ceremony. Ernie Muscat's eyes slid by me but did not stop. Maybe he thought I was just another Baptist observer.

The kids in the pews exchanged looks, as if seeking from

47

one another a cue on how to react to the strange ceremony they had just witnessed. The organ had not sounded, no hymns were sung. How oddly these Catholics worship God. But there was no snickering or lifted brows. Ecumenism is everywhere. Why don't Baptists make love standing up? So God won't think they're dancing. Maybe for a moment they feared the papists had come to reclaim their school.

The funeral director had taken over when I came out of the chapel, and Connolly's coffin on a wheeled cart was heading out the door. I held back until the procession was outside and then followed at a distance. Surely I had a right to be there. Why then did I feel like an interloper, almost a voyeur? The car I had rented was parked beside the road we walked on and, when I reached it, I was tempted to get in and drive away. What Nancy had said made me go on. She had called me Connolly's oldest friend. Perhaps there is always irony in the phrase. Can we be betrayed by strangers?

Most of the students who had been in chapel now followed the cortege as I was doing, at a distance, not really of it. They provided me with a disguise, but apparently I did not need one. No one had recognized me.

Over the wooden bridge that had always seemed oriental to me and up the path to the little mausoleum chapel on the island we went. The coffin was slid with some relief onto the rollers of the framework placed over the gaping grave. Lowry's voice was thinner in the open air. After he finished the graveside readings, he sprinkled the casket with holy water and then each of the priests did the same. Two girls beside me looked at one another. And then Muscat, in a loud voice, began to recite Psalm 129, in Latin. *"De profundis clamavi ad te, Domine; Domine, exaudi vocem meam."* He paused after the first verse and there was restless stirring among the clergy. Muscat began the second verse, slowly, waiting to be joined by the others.

Lowry took up the psalm, his voice hesitant, and then Muscat himself had trouble going on. He too had forgotten the psalm. The younger priests very likely had never prayed in Latin; it was doubtful they even knew the language. Muscat's botched effort summed up everything that had happened to the Church since Connolly and I had been students at Newman Hall.

I turned and walked back to my rented car, wanting to get the hell out of there.

Parked on the other side of the lake, I tried and failed to recite the psalm Muscat had wanted to say over the mortal remains of Connolly before they were lowered into the ground. "Out of the depths I have cried to thee, O Lord; Lord, hear my voice." I said the opening verse over and over, stressing the past tense. The roof of the school above the trees was a present object of perception but its significance for me lay far back on the line of time. It was more real in memory than in the present, and now my memories had lost their power because they would no longer be haunted by Michael Connolly.

I put the car in gear and pulled away. The last backward glance I cast at my old school seemed theatrical, played for an audience that was no more.

The parlor of the convent near Black River Falls was sparsely furnished. On the wall, a framed picture of St. Teresa of Avila wore a braided palm. Lilacs in a vase perfumed the air. On the other side of the grille, Sister Mary Rose of Lima, née Catherine Connolly, was barely discernible, a jigsaw puzzle whose pieces were not fitted closely enough together.

"I attended the funeral Mass in Washington, Sister. There was a great crowd."

"Our Mass that day was offered for the repose of his soul."

"Bishop Lowry officiated at the burial. Do you remember the island at Newman Hall?"

"No."

"You must. The three of us used to walk over there on visiting Sunday."

She nodded, acknowledging my memory but obviously not sharing it.

"The school has been sold to Protestants."

"Why was he buried there?"

"Apparently it was his wish."

Silence. "What are you doing now, James?"

Did she even remember me? She must, in some sense, or she would not have consented to come to the grille in the visiting parlor. She was immured in Carmel, a voluntary prisoner in a convent whose austere life would be repugnant to the majority of people—to the majority of nuns, for that matter. I thought of the days and weeks and years she had been there, the only events in her life the routine activities of the convent and the drama taking place in the depths of the soul she had given to God. I told her I now lived in Rome.

"Michael loved Rome."

"The city."

"Yes."

"When did you last see him?"

"In Advent. On Gaudete Sunday."

Last fall. "Sister, what did you think of him? Of his ideas?"

As I asked the question I had the odd thought that it was why I had come. On the drive there I had thought of the visit as paying my respects to the only family Connolly had left, but the changeless atmosphere of the Carmelite convent contrasted so vividly with the theological turmoil her brother had been involved in for so many years that I had to put the question to her. What I wanted, I suppose, was to hear Michael Connolly condemned by his holy sister.

"We never talked about his ideas," she said softly.

"Did you read his books?"

"No."

"Why not?"

"They did not seem written for us."

"But you did see them?"

"Michael always sent us copies."

"He was considered to be controversial." In that place the word sounded particularly idiotic.

"We talked of his soul."

It was my turn to be silent. The veiled figure on the other side of the grille was almost menacing, as if she could see into my soul and find it devoid of the faith that had once been there.

"So many have left the Church, Sister." Dear God, how phony my voice sounded, as if I were stating some lamentable fact.

"Have you?"

"Yes."

"You must pray."

"To whom, if I no longer believe?"

"To God. He is there. His existence does not depend upon your faith."

"Prayer does."

"Pray with me now."

She began to say the Lord's Prayer, slowly, the familiar words spoken with attention and devotion, whispered across the infinite space that separated us, though there was only the grille and perhaps two feet between my chair and hers. Simone Weil is said to have prayed the Our Father with total absorption and awe. Our Father. Had I ever said those words with the complete conviction that there is indeed a being whose loving concern for each of us surpasses that of an unimaginably devoted parent? Nothing in my past matched the conviction with which Sister Mary Rose of Lima said the prayer Jesus taught us. My lost faith had never had the valence of hers. I could not join in but sat there mute, not unlike the young priests at Connolly's grave when Muscat had intoned the "De profundis."

"I must go now. Pray for Michael."

"Pray for me, Sister."

She nodded and was gone. I leaned toward the grille and it was all I could do not to call her back. Twice in the same day the past receded from me as if now it was gone beyond retrieval.

The drive to Chicago took four hours, and throughout the trip I thought of the conversation in the convent parlor. Why had I told her I had lost my faith? She seemed to know the answer when she asked the question. Did I really think that Connolly's sister could peer into my soul? Did I even believe I had a soul for her to peer into? But my thoughts flew wide and far as I compared my life with that of the Carmelite nun. While I had traced tracks all over the globe she was confined in a convent near a small town in central Wisconsin. Sister Mary Rose of Lima believed that the history we create, whatever the range of our goings and comings, defines us for eternity, this life only the foyer of our eternal home, so that the only sensible course was to live for that promised future. On her own terms, she had chosen the better part. But even when I erased thoughts of heaven and hell, her life seemed more significant than the one I was leading.

The Illinois border freed me of such thoughts, and I resolved to put through a call to Rome from Chicago. My previous efforts to reach my apartment near the Campo di Fiori had been unsuccessful. What the hell was Maria doing?

Chapter 6

In New York I lunched with my agent Cassell and had several conferences with publishers during which I tried not to resent being treated like a fiction machine. But what else was I? Juvenile novels had provided me with a pleasant enough life, bouts of composition alternating with periods of leisure. My experience at *Alleluia* had prepared me for writing that is exhausted by a single reading, evanescent entertainment. Mine was an essentially commercial career, and though I had little appetite for the business side of writing, I had to pay attention to the views of those who bought my stuff. Gilligan, when I called him, was receptive to the idea of lunch.

"I go to the noon Mass at St. Patrick's. Why don't we meet there?"

"See you in church."

I arrived at twelve fifteen and stood in the back, trying to pick out Gilligan among the worshipers scattered through the vast nave. Manhattan had never struck me as a place conducive to prayer, and it was a surprise to see the number of people there. In the end, it was Gilligan who found me, suddenly appearing before me, dapper if a little bulgy. Outside we stood in the spring sunlight for a minute.

"Casey's all right with you, Jim?"

Casey's was fine. We ordered from a menu chalked on a board and sipped our oversized drinks.

"You're going back to Rome?"

I nodded. "It's home now."

"If I ever retire it will be to Ireland."

"I haven't retired."

"What are you doing?"

I saw no need for subterfuge with Gilligan, so I gave him the briefest of sketches of my career. If he disapproved, he gave no sign of it. He gave his slipping glasses the finger and looked around the bar.

"I'm trying to write a piece on Connolly. Without much success. That's something you should do, Jim. You knew him longer and better than anyone."

"Maybe longer, but not better. I saw him only rarely these past years."

"He did a lot of good." It seemed as much a question as a statement.

"I went out to Wisconsin for the burial, to our old school."

"Why don't you write that up for me?"

I smiled a noncommittal smile. How odd that during all the weeks since I had worked there, Gilligan had gone

on getting out issue after issue of *Alleluia*. He was a
symbol of stability, and I was aware of the distance I had
traveled since I worked for him. I would have been
embarrassed to tell Gilligan I no longer shared the faith
that took him to St. Patrick's every day at noon, no matter
my openness with Sister Mary Rose of Lima.

"It was good to see Nancy again," he said.

"Yes."

"Did you two get a divorce?"

"It's more definitive than that. Nancy got an annulment."

Gilligan knew the reason for my departure from Rome
and resignation from *Alleluia*, but it was like him to steer
clear of that.

"Tell me about Rome," he said cheerfully as our food
arrived. I did, and my life sounded interesting and full in
the telling. It is an old trick of fiction, to make the
humdum seem exciting.

Gilligan could not have gathered from my account that
I had had some troublesome discussions with Cassell and
my publishers. They had spoken of new trends in juvenile
writing, an emphasis on realism, and there were hints that
I was out of touch. Sales of my books were down dra-
matically. The night before, in my room at the Biltmore,
I had made ironic sketches of the kind of book they seemed
to want. The message was that juvenile novels had to be
more relevant, addressing the issues of the day, expanding
the consciousness of the reader, not mere entertainment.
Divorce, premarital sex, drugs, racism, that sort of thing.

NIP AND TUCK

The basic idea here is Willie's struggle for a sex change
operation against the opposition of his parents, sister and
bowling team while receiving the support he needs from his
pastor, who is short several sopranos in the church choir. A

5 5

tasteful but explicit opening scene is set in the boys' room at Pilgrim High. Willie is washing his hands at a sink while Herb Hubbert, star athlete, stands at a urinal. When Willie flees the room in tearful confusion, the reader is swept into the emotional trauma of a young person whose body may be male but whose longings are not. Thanks to moral stamina and the miracle of modern surgery, Willa, at story's end, takes her rightful place among the sopranos of the choir.

ALL IN THE FAMILY
Incest in an upper income WASP family with overtones of sadomasochism provides the theme. In the opening chapter, hung-over mother, still wearing her sleeping shade, takes into her arms her fourteen-year-old son under the (perhaps) mistaken impression he is her lover, the chauffeur, and the story gets off to a fast start. Climax in psychiatrist's office where Mom and Dad and the kids face up to their situation creatively.

I was not amused. I made my living writing stories for the young and if I was losing touch with my readers it was no laughing matter. Maybe I should not appear too indifferent to Gilligan's overtures.

I tried to imagine returning to *Alleluia*. Gilligan could bring Nancy back as well. With Connolly no longer a troubling presence on the edge of our lives, we might be able to make a new start, and this time do it right. Fantasy and dream. Would I want that if it were possible? Certainly Nancy would not. She had achieved an impressive independence during the past several years.

"I have no heir apparent," Gilligan said out of the blue.

"Neither do I."

Gilligan looked sad, remembering Gregory, and I despised myself for seeking sympathy. I lit a cigarette and Gilligan busied himself with his pipe.

"You should go back to Nancy, Jim."

"The annulment was her idea."

He ignored that. "Don't believe everything you hear."

"Like what?"

"People say vicious things. It seems to be a feature of the times. Michael Connolly had many enemies. In any case, he is dead now."

These words emerged enigmatically from a cloud of pipe smoke. Did he mean I no longer had a rival for Nancy's affection? He had said all he meant to say. Obviously Gilligan had heard the story Nose Bauer brought with him to Rome.

Back at the Biltmore I tried again to reach Maria in Rome but, as before, the phone in my apartment went unanswered. Finally I dialed her father's number, which I had looked up in O'Hare. A woman answered.

I said, "This is Professor Farragut at Loyola, and I am calling about Maria."

"Is there any further word?"

My God. "Then you've heard?"

"My husband left Sunday night. He doesn't trust foreign hospitals and—"

I hung up. Hospitals! It was as bad as I had begun to fear. Why had I left Maria the use of my car? This seemed the obvious source of whatever had happened. I decided against calling Salvator Mundi, the hospital on the Janiculum favored by Americans. They would tell me nothing. I had to get back. My return flight did not leave for two days, and I was booked out of Dulles. Changing flights presented no problem since I had paid full fare. My passport, however, did.

It was not in my suitcase. It was not on my person. I must have left it at Nancy's, with all but one of my credit cards. The cards I knew I had left with her, in the bag that had been filled with European newspapers. I put through a call to Nancy but she did not answer, nor could I locate her at the offices of the Bishops Conference. She had not come in to work that day. The alarming news about Maria —I knew enough to know the news was bad—and the absence of my passport made me eager to be on my way. Think. Passport. State Department. Washington. My flight would leave from Dulles. By applying for a new passport in Washington I could eliminate the middle man and be able to leave for Europe as soon as I got it. If I had left it in Nancy's apartment, I could certainly be on my way the following morning.

In LaGuardia I had half an hour that I spent on the phone trying to learn the fastest way to replace a passport.

"You mean you want to renew your passport?"

"No. Replace it. I've lost mine."

"Was it still valid?"

"That's right."

"You'll have to come in. With photographs."

"How long will it take?"

"That varies. No more than a couple days."

"I was hoping for something faster. I'm due back in Rome. At the moment, I'm on my way to Washington. Can I get a passport more quickly there?"

The woman seemed to be chewing something. Her tone was laconic; I had not fully engaged her interest.

"You're going back to Rome." She sighed.

"That's right."

"Lucky you."

"Have you been there?"

"Oh, yes." Her voice was heavy with suggestive intonations. "I'd love to go back."

"Planes leave every day."

"Sure. And astronauts go to the moon."

"How long has it been since you were in Rome?"

The booth I was in was one of half a dozen opposite the ticket counter. Lines of passengers stood patiently to check their baggage and get seat assignments. In airports it is difficult to retain the romantic sense of travel the woman on the phone obviously had. She was trying to remember exactly how long it had been since her European trip. The conversation was crazy, but what is not? Forty-four, cuckold, my marriage annulled, my best friend dead and my professional career in vague jeopardy, eager to get back to a girl half my age, I spoke on the phone with a stranger. In fifteen minutes I would hop the shuttle to Washington. In the meantime why not let this unknown woman bore me with the slide show of her memories?

When I got to Washington I could not discover if my passport was at Nancy's because I could not reach her either at home or at work. The telephone was an instrument of impotence, a device through which I could not get in contact with women. I scowled into the camera at the photographer's and, armed with a little envelope of prints, headed for the passport office. No problem. My new passport would be ready by nightfall. The woman who waited on me had a long upper lip, a gummy smile, and eyes that seemed pressured from below when she smiled. There is some unhealthy ratio of women to men in Washington, making things tough even for attractive women. This poor thing would have been safe in the Navy, as we used to say, but she was pleasant and efficient. Perhaps in the ages of faith she would have been a nun.

The best I could do by way of a room was a motel far out on Massachusetts Avenue, practically on the campus of Catholic University. I felt I had come full circle when the cab went past the Shrine of the Immaculate Conception. There was a high cyclone fence bordering the driveway of the motel, and we came into what seemed a compound where the blue-green pool sparkled in the sunlight. The thought that the place was safe made me feel unsafe.

My room was poorly lit and smelled vaguely of urine, though that might have been a disinfectant, the cure worse than the disease. Nancy still did not answer her phone. Although I had a new passport and would be able to board the morning plane, I would have liked a farewell meal with my not-quite-former wife. Her unanswered phone now seemed a refusal. There was nothing to do but worry about Maria. Don't let her be injured. Keep her safe.

Who was the addressee of these hopes? I will not call them prayers. My hopes had nothing to do with the purity of motive that animated the words of a Sister Mary Rose of Lima. In a room in the Holiday Inn in Washington, amid floral drapes, Italianate furniture made of pine, two double beds and a smell of urine, I reflected that in convents and monasteries all over the world, around the clock, contemplatives prayed for the rest of us. I hoped they could help Maria now.

"What are you doing way out there?" Nancy asked when I got through to her much later that night. There was an odd excitement in her voice.

"I didn't have any choice."

"You sound funny."

"I had a few drinks."

"When do you leave for Rome?"

Couldn't she wait? "That's why I'm calling. I leave in the morning."

"I'd hoped we would see each other again."

"What are you doing now?"

"It's after eleven o'clock."

"I can come there."

There was a pause whose length did not flatter. "Won't there be time in the morning?"

"No."

She agreed. Leaving the armed camp of the motel—there

6 o

were security guards scattered here and there: in the lobby, near the cabana, at the driveway's entrance where the gate had to be opened—I had the irrational thought that it was Nancy's fault I was staying in such a place.

Once more she stood in her open door when I got off the elevator. Her expression was the serene Madonna one I remembered from the year she was unfaithful to me. I felt watched from a height whose perspective made me slightly comic.

"I'm not drunk," I assured her.

"Would you like a drink?"

I refused. We were fencing, and I did not know why. I told her about the passport.

"I'm sure it's not here. Do you want to look?"

It wasn't. Neither were my credit cards. I would have sworn I had left them in a bag in her spare room, but the bag was missing too.

"It doesn't matter. I've been issued a new passport."

Nancy sat under the photograph of our son. Assuming she would want to know of the Wisconsin trip, I began at the end, with my visit to Connolly's sister, but when I started to tell her of the ceremony at Newman Hall, Nancy stopped me.

"It was really very tasteful," I assured her.

"I don't want to hear about it." She smiled oddly.

"Suit yourself."

She leaned forward and studied me carefully. "Jim, something incredible has happened."

"Tell me about it."

She hesitated. The odd smile came and went. "Jim, he was here. I've seen him."

"Whom have you seen?"

I was aware of the buzz of an electric clock on the table

next to me; from outside came the faint sounds of traffic. She looked intently at me with her wide-spaced eyes. Her lips were parted; she invited some response I could never give.

"I saw Michael Connolly. He was here in this apartment."

Part Two

Chapter 1

When I checked in for my flight the following day, Gilligan and a thin elderly man who looked familiar were in line just ahead of me. Momentarily, I had the wild hope that Gilligan would be on my flight, but it turned out that he was in Washington on business. How I would have liked to talk with someone who knew Nancy. But it was Gilligan's companion, a man named Furey, who would be boarding with me.

"Clark was on the staff of *Alleluia*," Gilligan said, and Furey scowled. "He was here for the funeral."

"You've buried the magazine?" Furey brightened.

"Michael Connolly's funeral."

"Oh, yes." Furey's manner grew brighter still. "In saner times that man would have been burned at the stake."

"Is Nancy here to see you off?" Gilligan asked.

If we had been alone, I might have seized the opportunity to tell Gilligan what Nancy had said to me the night before. Until I communicated it to someone else, I would feel tainted by her madness. Nancy claimed that a man who had been solemnly commemorated in Washington and buried in Wisconsin had walked into her apartment alive. Could I burden even Gilligan with that story?

I said, "She works. That's why she didn't go to Wisconsin."

"Jim attended Connolly's burial in Wisconsin," Gilligan explained to Furey.

"May he rest in peace and all that," Furey said. "But the man was a sower of confusion in the Church. I cannot regret his passing."

"Don't be so severe, Harry," Gilligan said quietly.

"Connolly was the beneficiary of leniency and indecision. He should have been silenced years ago."

I had now placed Harold Furey. He was the executive director of the Crusader Foundation and presided over the distribution of fifteen million dollars annually. One of Gilligan's dreams was that Furey would provide a subsidy that would reduce the loss *Alleluia* incurred every year. That wan hope must have brought him to Washington. Each man was the single ideological opposite personally known by the other. Furey might not want to burn Gilligan at the stake, but he would cheerfully preside over the burning of *Alleluia*. But then Gilligan thought people like Furey should be declared excommunicate for their denial of the social gospel.

"He is silent now," Gilligan said.

I glanced at him. What would he make of Nancy's crazy

claim to have seen Connolly after his burial? What would anyone say? My own reaction had been anger.

"Jimmy, I mean it. He was here."

Her tone was breathless, her eyes alight. This was a different Nancy from the woman who had invited me to spend the night before Connolly's memorial in her apartment. Then her manner had been the stoic resignation of a pagan, as if Connolly's death had made her posthumous. Now she was vibrant with an almost sexual excitement. I got to my feet.

"You don't believe me." She spoke as if I had just contradicted some self-evident truth. "You don't believe me," she repeated sadly. O ye of little faith.

"Nancy, I saw Michael buried in Wisconsin. He died, remember?"

She nodded, as if to a slow learner. "Nonetheless he was here."

"And what great news did he bring you from the beyond?"

"At first I was hysterical. He frightened me half to death."

"Only half? What stopped you from going all the way?"

This inadvertent use of a phrase from our youth— "going all the way" meant that a girl could be made— increased my anger. I could not ignore the jealousy I felt.

"Jimmy, sit down and listen."

I shook my head. She was trying to make me an accomplice, and I would have nothing to do with that. Whatever stunt she was attempting, I did not like it. She had conjured up the ghost of Connolly to breathe new life into herself. I opened the door and she crossed the room and put a hand on my arm.

"Jimmy, he stood right where you're standing now and . . ."

I shook off her hand and stepped into the hall. She was

crazy, of course, but I was unnerved by the conviction of her manner, the awed way she spoke of Connolly, her general aspect of being one of those Marys at the empty tomb. Any affection I had felt for her over lunch in Georgetown was gone. Nancy was the woman who had betrayed me and now wanted me to rejoice that her lover had come back from the grave to visit her.

Because she remained in her doorway, I could not wait for the elevator. My last glimpse of her was of a saddened yet eerily contented woman. This betrayal was worse than the original one.

I had walked for several blocks down the deserted streets before I remembered that it is unsafe to be out alone at night in Washington, D.C. Between street lamps the stars were visible, but any shadow might conceal a mugger. I left the sidewalk and went into the street. How silent it was. I could half believe that the late Michael Connolly had come along this way to visit Nancy, materializing out of the darker night into which he had gone. An approaching car turned its lights off and on, and I retreated to the side of the street. The driver apparently considered me fair game. The car headed directly at me. I hopped onto the curb but the headlights did not veer away. Fear was an almost welcome emotion after what I had felt with Nancy. The car came to a stop beside me, and a flashlight shone in my eyes. Did muggers now work from automobiles? Blinded, I heard a car door slam. I would have run, but my legs were weak beneath me.

"Let's see your identification."

It was a cop, visible now in the light his companion behind the wheel trained on me. Leather and metal, law and order. I could have cried out in relief. As I pulled out my wallet, I realized the officer had drawn his pistol. He took my wallet and flipped it open.

"You James Clark?"

"That's right."

"Are you drunk?"

"No! I had a drink or two, but I'm not drunk."

"Why are you walking in the street?"

"I was frightened."

"Of what?"

"Muggers. I don't know."

"Where is this address?" He tried to say it.

"Rome."

"Italy?"

"I live there. Look, I've been visiting my wife. My ex-wife."

"Where does she live?"

The thought of going back to Nancy's in the custody of the police had no appeal. "I'm staying at the Holiday Inn out on Massachusetts Avenue. That's where I'm going. I want a cab."

The flashlight went off. My wallet was handed back to me. The officer hesitated, then said, "Get into the car."

"Are you arresting me?"

"We'll take you to a cab stand."

Throughout the drive, they ignored me. I babbled, giving them my reason for returning from Rome, mentioned having gone to Wisconsin and New York. They had lost all interest in me. In the event, it was not necessary for them to take me to a cab stand. A taxi waiting for a light was empty, and the cop behind the wheel gave a little toot of his horn. The cabbie's angry look turned to guilty surprise. The cop who had checked my wallet rolled down his window.

"We've got a fare for you."

I transferred to the cab. The light changed, and we started off. The driver was looking at me in his mirror.

"Jesus, what was that all about?"

I gave him the name of the motel. My urge to talk had left me. "I hitched a ride," I said.

"Jesus."

At the motel, I went into the lounge and had two drinks in rapid succession, but ice water would have had as much effect on me. The farther I got from Nancy, the angrier I became at her goddam romantic hallucinations. Michael came to see me. He was here. Jesus, as the cabbie would have said.

Sometime during the night I woke up and could not get to sleep again. For a moment I feared I was going to have a migraine. I tried my left side, then my right, then lay on my back staring at the ceiling and listening to the weird muffled sounds of nighttime Washington. I propped up my pillow and, feeling no signs of an impending headache, lit a cigarette. Nancy and I used to share a cigarette in bed after we had made love, the lit end glowing when we dragged on it, passing it back and forth. In silence. No need to talk. I dragged on my cigarette now, making the memory more real. In the dead of night, alone in a motel bed, it is easy to feel sorry for oneself. The rest of the world is sealed away beyond other walls, behind locked doors, and I was absurdly certain that in all the other beds men and women lay in each other's arms or shared a cigarette, sated and at peace, as Nancy and I had done.

When I first met her she still had the look of a nun, but, outside the convent walls, she was receptive to the world, intent on eradicating any guilt she felt at putting behind her a life of consecrated virginity. She wanted relevance, using the word as an absolute, and she still saw her life through the lens of faith. If she had left one vocation, she was looking for another. Something intellectual. That is why she had come to *Alleluia* looking for a job. Gilligan turned her over to me.

"What do you do here?" she asked. Her reaction when

I told her I was a writer gave me an intimation of what Pulitzer Prize winners must feel.

"I did some writing in college," she said.

At *Alleluia* one began at the bottom, but that was not so far from the top. Nancy did copyediting, she corrected proofs, she began to review books. Within six months, she wrote a publishable article, or so I thought, but Gilligan turned it down.

"Ex-nuns." He shook his head. He meant the subject of her article, not Nancy. "It is well written though."

"She has something to say, Gilly."

He moved papers about on his desk and avoided my eye. He knew I was taking Nancy out and seemed to think this disqualified my judgment of her work. His search was rewarded. He held up a piece of paper on which he had scrawled a note to himself.

"Have her try a thousand words on this."

In the end, Nancy did three articles on the underground liturgy at a seminary out on Long Island. She went out there and interviewed, talking with students and faculty and one wary monsignor in the chancery office. It established her at *Alleluia*. And *Commonweal* took her piece on ex-nuns.

We celebrated at a Japanese restaurant, still a novelty in those days, and cheap. Nancy insisted on using chopsticks, as if she felt that any obstacle could be overcome. Our waitress, in native costume, prepared our meal before our very eyes and we ate like conspirators. I knew how Nancy felt. She had conquered New York. She was a writer. So what if all that meant was that she was on the staff of *Alleluia*?

When we came outside snow was drifting down, huge flakes fluttering in the lights, turning Manhattan into a small town. Hand in hand we walked to Broadway, where we caught a cab to 16th Street, where she had a walkup apartment in a building where all the doors had double locks at least. The week before a man had been murdered on the street below her window in what the French are pleased to call a crime of passion. Nancy turned her radio to an FM station that played semiclassical music with a minimum of commercials, and we sat on her couch and smoked. Not counting the diminutive kitchen, she had two rooms, the one we sat in and her bedroom.

"I love your shirts," she said. I had taken off my jacket and tie. She ran a hand over my shirt, then put her face to my chest and inhaled.

"What's wrong with my socks?"

"Why do they starch them?"

"My socks?"

She punched me. "Did I ever tell you how we starched and ironed our wimples?"

"Don't."

She looked up at me and her smile faded. The lid of her left eye drooped slightly, her nose was narrow at the bridge and her hair, parted in the middle, fell bell-like on either side of her face.

"Author, author," I whispered.

And she lifted her face to my kiss.

We did not sleep together before we married. The question simply never arose, no matter how passionately we might embrace and kiss by the hour on her couch. It was a matter of upbringing. My love for her was exquisitely chaste. I told her that I had loved her since the first moment she had walked into the offices of *Alleluia*.

"Me too."

No one was surprised when we announced we were going to marry. Gilligan gave a reception for us at the office after the ceremony in a little chapel a block from the Biltmore, our nuptial Mass witnessed by a dozen friends and the tourists who come and go continuously there. We honeymooned in the Barclay, taking a week off, then settled into her apartment. Three months after the wedding, Nancy was pregnant and we began to talk of moving to a house. We found a duplex in Queens.

In the Holiday Inn in Washington years later, smoking a lonely cigarette and remembering those early months of our marriage, I came dangerously close to crying. But Nancy's claim to have seen the dead Michael Connolly broke my mood. I stubbed out my cigarette and memories of my wife.

"He'll never give you a cent," I told Gilligan in the waiting room at Dulles. Furey had gone to take a leak, his very words. Gilligan's pipe was unlit. He nodded.

"I know that. Harry's idea of benefiting humanity is to hire planes to dump holy cards on the Congo."

"You're kidding."

"Just exaggerating. His current interest is the canonization of Margaret Rusher."

"Who's she?"

"God knows. So you're going back to Rome."

"Do you ever see Nancy?"

"Only at funerals."

There was the opportunity I had thought I wanted. But I did not want to tell Gilly Nancy's nutty story of having been visited by Connolly. Her guilty secret was safe with me. Gilly knew about her and Connolly because I had told him, ignoring the obvious pain the story gave him. The editor of *Alleluia* did not want to believe that his fellow soldiers in the armies of *aggiornamento* were capable of such shenanigans. He had the veteran Catholic's unwillingness to believe scandal where the clergy is concerned, though such matters were a regular item in the news of the day. The torrent of laicizations had just begun.

"What should I do, Gilly?"

"Seventy times seven," he murmured.

Forgive her? But then Gilligan was a bachelor. I suppose it all sounded like the Miller's Tale to him. Maybe that is what it was. Chaucer's betrayed husband, hoisted in a tub to the ceiling, waiting for the flood, was no more foolish than I.

"Say hello to the pope," Gilligan said when Furey hove into view. I left the old enemies to themselves, wondering at Gilligan's kindness at coming to see Furey off. He did not need me to tell him that he would never receive the subsidy that would keep *Alleluia* afloat. Maybe the magazine was destined to sink now, having fulfilled the small role it had played when we had all been so sure that the Council meant a new day for the Church. I wondered if Gilly could admit even now, in his heart of hearts, that what we had witnessed, and contributed to, was the dissolution of Catholicism. It was doubtful in the extreme that he found the new liturgy and antinomian theology to his liking. His heroes were Frank Sheed and Maisie Ward, George Shuster and the old *Commonweal* crowd. Yet, as I had seen, he still attended daily Mass and received communion as he always had. Maybe it was that he and Furey had in common, a shared solid piety beneath the obvious differences between them.

Furey had an aisle seat directly across from mine, which was bad enough, but when it became clear that I had three seats to myself and he had half a row of children with him in the center of the cabin, he asked if he could join me.

"They should be in nonsmoking anyway," he growled as he took the window seat. He meant the children, who watched him change seats with widened eyes. Their mother was delighted and proceeded to make a nest of the

7 4

six seats she now had for her brood. A cigarette dangled from her mouth, solving Furey's small puzzle.

When I sat down again, I opened the Agatha Christie I had bought in Dulles, motivated by more than a wish for diversion. Cassell had given me a sense of unease, and I could half believe that I had run out the string with juvenile books. What then? To dig I was not able, to beg I was ashamed. Could I perhaps write mysteries? Writing was all I really knew. I wished I had explored the possibility of Rome correspondent for *Alleluia* when I had Gilligan alone.

"I've read them all," Furey said, nodding at my book. "Agatha Christie."

"Are there many?"

"Not enough for me."

That seemed an omen. If even Furey read mysteries, the market must be good indeed. Once back in Rome, I would give the matter serious thought and then query Cassell on the prospects.

The usual busy commotion preceding a transatlantic flight went on. We were provided with menus, a flight attendant began to hawk earphones. I rented a set, not because I wanted to see the movie, but because it would be another defense against talking with Furey. To my surprise, he too paid for earphones. He had been studying the airline magazine and showed me the list of canned programs.

"I like the comic routines."

"Do you get to Europe often?"

He nodded. "Gilligan tells me you live in Rome."

"That's right."

"I envy you. I mean to retire there." Furey looked to be in his late sixties or early seventies. What little hair he had left was white and stood up in patches on his narrow skull. The backs of his hands were spotted, an old man's hands. I wondered when he thought he would be ready for retirement. "A small apartment near the Vatican, maybe even a hotel, to simplify the meal situation. Where do you live?"

I told him, going into more detail than I had intended, and his eyes glazed with disinterest. He snapped open the plastic bag containing his earphones and without apology plugged them in and clamped them on his head. I was dismissed.

Head back, eyes closed, I feigned sleep, and then real sleep came. When I awoke, we were in flight. Beside me Furey was laughing silently in response to the jokes he was listening to. There was a drink on his tray. I unbuckled and went forward to where the flight attendants congregated in a galley and asked for bourbon on the rocks. The plane was perhaps three-quarters full and I could easily have changed seats, but there seemed no point in that with Furey engrossed in comic routines and the children across the aisle drowsy and quiet, thanks to the Dramamine their mother had given them. Sipping my drink, I looked out the porthole in the emergency door opposite the galley. Far below cloud cover obscured the sea. I went back to my seat.

Furey looked up at me with an idiot grin but did not remove his earphones. I settled down with my drink and tried unsuccessfully to read Agatha Christie. She did not provide any model I might imitate should I try my hand at mysteries. When our meal was served, Furey became sociable again.

"So you worked for Gilligan at *Alleluia?*"

"For nearly five years."

"I never read it."

"Not many people do anymore."

"Good. Gilligan is an old friend of mine and I do not

wish him harm, but that magazine stands for a good part of what is wrong with the Church nowadays."

"You didn't approve of the Council?"

The question set him off, first on a distinction between the Council and what people like Gilligan and Connolly had persuaded people it said, and then on to the shambles Holy Mother Church now found herself in. He went through the whole familiar litany, the crazy Masses one was subjected to, mad nuns and madder priests, defiance of Rome and the bishops, a loss of the sense of the supernatural. He had ordered veal parmigiana and ate with relish as he tolled the bell of doom.

"You actually made a special trip to attend Connolly's funeral?" With a plastic spoon he was trying to get the last of his custard out of its cup.

"We were boyhood friends."

"Was he always a heretic?"

I laughed, but Furey was serious.

"Whatever his intentions, that is what he was. A heretic." He brought a baby carrot to his mouth and clamped his teeth on it. Chewing, he said, "He was summoned to Rome, you know."

"I know."

"They should have condemned him then. Not that it would have done much good. That would have made him even more of a hero to the press. To people who don't give a good goddam about the fate of the Church. He catered to them."

"He's dead," I said, but I might have been rejecting Nancy's crazy claim rather than placating Furey.

"Yes. I wonder what he thinks now, standing before the throne of God, when he remembers all the nonsense he wrote."

Furey obviously took pleasure in the image of Michael Connolly getting a celestial chewing out for all the confusion he had caused. Was his belief in a divine judgment taking place even higher than we then were any less absurd than Nancy's claim to have been visited by a dead man?

"Why did you stop working for Gilligan?"

"It's a long story."

"Did you see the light or what?"

"Nothing so dramatic as that."

"What do you do in Rome?"

"I'm a writer."

Furey looked at me in silence. If I had been a used car he would have kicked my tires. "I'll be staying at the Hassler. Look me up."

"How long will you be in Rome?"

"I'm planning on two weeks. Maybe more." He lit a multifiltered cigarette and smoke rose swiftly to the little vent above him. "Gilligan spoke very highly of you."

Would Gilly have told him my marriage had gone sour and that was why I sent in my resignation to *Alleluia*? It was possible, I suppose, but that would not have interested Furey in me. On the contrary. Well, I had no intention of looking him up at the Hassler. Furey had Knights of Malta business to attend to among other things. From the Hassler, high above the Spanish Steps, he could look down at the flag of his order fluttering over a palazzo on the Via Condotti. He could also look across the Tiber to the hotel in which Nancy had betrayed me, within walking distance of the Vatican, a location of the kind Furey dreamt of for his retirement.

My earphones were still in their plastic bag when the lights were turned off and the movie began. I tipped back my seat and closed my eyes, preferring the drama on the screen of memory.

On the Borgo Pio, near a fountain to which people in

the neighborhood came for their water, there is a little hostaria with half a dozen outside tables under an awning. Nancy and Connolly and I often had lunch together there during the Council. The tables were square and wobbly, the pasta good, the wine abundant, and we sat on into the sleepy afternoon talking. Nancy would have spent the morning painting while Connolly and I had been to briefings or waiting for the morning session in St. Peter's to end, and the three of us felt we had earned our indolence. That Connolly liked Nancy was pleasant to me; he was genuinely interested in her painting and was quick to encourage her on days when it was going badly and she was morose. Nancy saw Connolly as the star of the Council. His articles were drawing sophisticated attention at home, and he had set the tone for coverage of the sessions. I was proud to be able to produce so important a friend. Soon we were all friends, and both Nancy and I were flattered that Connolly preferred our company to the more dazzling lunches he might have been enjoying.

The day things began to go wrong, we had been talking of celibacy. Connolly was certain its days were numbered.

"We will live to see married priests. You can bet on it."

"Have you anyone particular in mind?"

My question drew a frown from Nancy. Celibacy was too serious a matter to be treated with levity. Perhaps she could feel better about having left the convent if chastity and celibacy became dead letters.

"It's not a personal matter for me," Connolly said.

"Just the principle of the thing?"

He smiled. "Why is it always married men who rise to the defense of a celibate priesthood?"

"Who's defending it? Why should priests be happy?"

Another attempt at humor gone awry. Nancy's mouth became a line. She inhaled through her nose and then was almost audibly silent. That swiftly she became a long-suffering wife and I the obtuse husband. Connolly, unaware of this, hunched over the table.

"We have to realize just how exciting these times are. The Church can make more progress in a few years than in the previous three hundred. We have a long way to go. That's why it is so important to prevent old bastards like Ottaviani from twisting the Council to their own purposes."

Nancy forgot her pique with me and listened, enraptured, as Connolly made a rapid sketch of the New Jerusalem awaiting us if only the liberal forces at the Council were permitted to work their will. He made no secret of his partisanship in the articles he sent back to New York, which is why they were so popular. His secular readers were presented with a Church on the verge of throwing off its medieval and counter-Reformation shackles and entering the modern world. That world does not understand unmarried priests or nuns buried away in convents, and Connolly enabled its inhabitants to think that, on all crucial points, they were right and the Church was wrong.

"What does Catherine think of that?" I asked.

"Who's Catherine?"

I let Connolly answer Nancy's question. Did I detect the slightest relief when she learned that Catherine was his sister? I lifted the wine carafe, but Connolly put a hand over his glass. Nancy hesitated, then did the same. I refilled my own glass and drank half of it. A thin cat approached the fountain, hopped up onto its rim, and began to lap delicately at the standing water.

"We were never cloistered," Nancy said.

"Carmelites are a different matter," Connolly said. "Most of the other orders are engaged in work anyone could do."

"And do better." Nancy shook a cigarette free and Connolly lit it for her. "If I had stayed I would have ended up teaching grade school."

"Exactly. It was cheap labor. That was the main attraction for pastors. Well, from now on parochial schools are going to have to pay their staffs a living wage."

I did not find it easy to think of the nuns I had had in grade school as an exploited group of women. Theirs had been a dedicated life, a holy life. I did find it hard to imagine Nancy as one of them. Nor did I even faintly disapprove of her decision not to become a nun. But, drinking wine and watching the cat which now lay in the shadow of the fountain, I disliked hearing her talk as if leaving the convent was a more serious decision than staying would have been. Connolly encouraged her sense that she had made the better choice, nodding in agreement with any banality she uttered, and I thought of her on our balcony plugging away all morning at her easel.

We were the last to leave the hostaria. I had an appointment with a monsignor who lived in one of the huge elegant apartment buildings that flank the Via della Conciliazione, so we parted in the street. Nancy and Connolly went off in the direction of our hotel while I started up the Borgo Pio toward the gate of the Vatican, where a Swiss guard stood at easy attention. I stopped and looked back.

Nancy and Connolly were still visible, walking slowly, still talking animatedly, a man and woman alone on an afternoon street in Rome. I shaded my eyes against the sun and watched them out of sight. When I turned back toward the Vatican gate, my head light with wine, I was ashamed of the jealousy the sight of my wife with Michael Connolly stirred up in me.

For two weeks I was afflicted with the thought that

Connolly's interest was in Nancy, not me. His glamour and prominence, the fact that it was inconceivable one could ever be bored by him, made me by contrast even dimmer than I was, nor did it seem consolation enough that, as a priest, as a celibate, he could not be my rival for Nancy. The thought that filled me with depression was that, if Nancy had had a choice between the two of us, she would not have hesitated for a minute. Did she, in imagination, dream of a past contrary to fact, replace her pedestrian husband with the dazzling Connolly? Doubt and suspicion, once admitted, are not easily expelled from the mind.

From then on, when the three of us were together, I could not resist taking the view opposite to Connolly's. Inevitably, Nancy sided with him and I was wounded by what I considered her disloyalty. In sickness and in health, in stupidity and childishness . . . Once I even rose to the defense of Cardinal Ottaviani, whose objections to the new canon of the Mass suddenly seemed full of merit to me.

"What's wrong with you?" Nancy and I were sitting at midnight on our balcony, a vast star-streaked sky above us, enjoying relief from the heat of the day.

"Is something wrong with me?"

"You keep arguing with Michael."

"We're old friends. We've always argued."

"It's childish. You don't mean what you say."

"Maybe we're seeing too much of him."

Silence. And then, "I don't think I could bear Rome if we didn't see him as often we do."

It was a moment when I might have said something awful, words bubbling forth from my jealous heart, but I managed to remain silent. To say what I thought would have made things infinitely worse. Nancy put out her cigarette and went inside, but I remained on the balcony.

When I finally did go in, she was in bed, asleep. The sound of her regular breathing seemed an insult, as if she had rebuffed advances I meant to make. I returned to the balcony and tried to sleep sitting in a chair. That proved impossible. Finally I joined her in bed, but I lay as far from her as I could, on the very edge, as if I were punishing her. I wished that I had become a Trappist or a Carthusian, a hermit whose only relations were with God.

I was freed of my silly suspicions by seeing Connolly saying Mass. Vested, at the main altar of Santa Susanna, he was quite simply a priest. My jealousy went so swiftly and completely that I could not believe I had really doubted Nancy. Not that I had imagined anything remotely sexual between them. Nancy was the only woman I had ever slept with, and she had been a virgin when we married. For either of us to engage in what we did together with anybody else was simply unthinkable. It was not an idea that occurred and was then rejected; it was an idea that could not even begin to form in the mind. Of what then had I been jealous? Her mind, her heart, her soul. That her love might be divided and a greater share of it directed elsewhere was the possibility that had devastated me. But Connolly in chasuble and alb, celebrating Mass at Santa Susanna, no longer seemed my spiritual rival.

A Wednesday. A midmorning briefing of the press at a time when there was a lull in the final session of the Council. Not many of my fellow journalists had even bothered to show up. Connolly was not there, but then he did not frequent such set-piece affairs. His preference was for the private source, the talkative insider, the *peritus* with a grudge. His articles were full of references to informants who could not be named. This made what he wrote difficult to refute, and more than once a rival journalist had suspected he invented at least half of his mysterious sources. That morning I felt boringly conscientious. I had never missed a press briefing. I was always present at any event that could claim a measure of relevance to my obligations as *Alleluia*'s Council correspondent. This unimaginative dutifulness did not, however, improve my prose or make my articles better. And so, before it was over, I slipped away from the briefing.

How is it that one walk along a way I had gone a thousand times should remain so vivid when it was only in retrospect that it took on significance? At a newsstand in the shadow of the Bernini colonnade I picked up my newspapers: *Il Tempo, Corriere della Sera, Le Monde* and *Figaro,* the *Herald Tribune* and the *Rome Daily American.* The *London Observer* was a Sunday treat. On tables around the kiosk were assorted guides to the Vatican and Rome in various languages and the miniature Pietàs and busts of John XXIII no one ever seemed to buy. When I came from shadow into sunlight the little piazza was filled with blocky green buses whose exhaust fumes seemed a reminder of mortality. The April day seemed kind, with the promise of noontime meals already emanating from the open doors of restaurants. I stopped for a cappuccino and drank it standing at the bar, my papers under my arm. If I thought of anything, it was that I did not want to interrupt Nancy at her painting. Did I, when I passed "our" hostaria, think of the absurd jealousy that had begun at a table there? How incredible my suspicions would have seemed to me that day.

Our hotel occupied the terrazzo and the three upper floors of a building whose intermediate floors contained offices and apartments and one dentist whose ineptitude I could verify by running my tongue over the tooth he had filled. As usual, the elevator did not come when I pressed the button. *Occupato.* Unless its double doors were fully closed it would not budge, and they had to be closed by hand. I started up the marble stairs, which wound round the screened shaft of the elevator, hoping that the car was not stalled on the top floor. I found it three floors up, its doors still open. When I stepped in, it wobbled under my weight. My face in the mirror wore a smile. Wouldn't Nancy be surprised to see me home so soon?

The door of our room was locked, of course, and my first knock went unanswered. Nancy, out on the balcony, would not easily hear it. I knocked again, loudly, and tried to whisper her name in a shout. Still no answer. It occurred to me that she might have gone out, and I felt stupid for not checking at the desk to see if our key was there. I must have stood outside the locked door for five minutes before I decided to go downstairs for the key. The elevator was still at our floor. I noticed that I had not shut the doors tightly and included myself among those I had cursed earlier.

There were three preoccupied clerks behind the desk and, typically, none of them noticed me at once. It was infra dig to be overtly considerate of a guest. I had already seen that our key was not on its hook. The clerk who finally acknowledged my presence did not know if Signora had gone out. He consulted his colleagues and they shared his ignorance. And indifference. There was a phone on the counter and I could have rung the room but did not; these languid functionaries put me on my own dignity. I went across the hall to the lounge and settled down with my papers.

From where I sat I had a diagonal look at the elevator, which was between me and the short flight of steps leading down to the street entrance. Minutes after I had sat down Michael Connolly emerged from the elevator and hurried across the lobby to those stairs. His furtive speed was eloquent with guilt. He did not see me. How long did it take before he was gone? I was conscious that I was living in a moment that divided my life forever into two parts.

My first thought was that one of the clerks at the desk would have seen Connolly leave and made the inference I had. Only it was not an inference. I knew with infallible certainty that Connolly had been with Nancy in our room and that what I had considered my childish jealousy was in fact a kind of clairvoyance. I could not move. I sat there holding *Le Monde* just as I had been doing when Connolly fled into the street. Would anyone watching me have guessed that I had just suffered a mortal wound?

When feeling returned, it was shame I felt, not anger. I folded my papers carefully, rose and crossed the lobby to the stairs. Walking was an activity I seemed to have to put my mind to, as if it were something I must learn how to do again. Nothing was familiar and routine now. At the bottom of the stairs, I hesitated before going into the street. I dreaded the possibility that I might see Connolly, and then I could not resist going out and looking up and down the street for him. But he was nowhere in sight. Which way would he have gone? I wanted to take the opposite direction. Confronting him with what I knew was the last thing I wished to do. No more did I want to go upstairs to Nancy. I walked slowly up the Borgo to what I had thought of as our hostaria, sat at a table with my back to the wall and ordered a *mezzo litro* of wine. Red wine. I preferred red wine. I no longer had to defer to the preferences of others. The waiter brought bread with the wine, and I realized he thought I had come for an early lunch. It was scarcely half past eleven.

When I began to feel the effect of the wine, I tried to believe that I was mistaken about the significance of Connolly's being with Nancy. I imagined them leaning over

8 6

the balcony, looking out across the rooftops, talking inno-
cently until my knock at the door had altered the scene.
It was even possible Connolly had been somewhere else
in the hotel, or on one of those floors of the building
where lawyers and my dentist plied their trades. Perhaps
one of his secret sources lived there. I did not even want
to believe any of these implausible accounts. The attempt
to do so would have been refuted by the way Connolly
had left the hotel.

I thought of Gregory, of course. Nancy had betrayed
him as well. My dead son became my ally in grief. So did
the wine. I had all but finished the half liter when Nancy
joined me.

"Have you ordered?" she asked, pulling out a chair.

"Not yet."

"Is Michael coming?"

"I don't know." The waiter approached. "I haven't
seen him."

She took the menu, an illegible hectagraphed thing,
and studied it. She ordered a salad and risotto con funghi.
She loved rice, a fact I had first learned when we celebrated her debut as a writer in that Japanese restaurant
in Manhattan.

"Was he at the briefing?"

"No."

She lit a cigarette, and there was no telltale trembling
of her hand when she held the match. At the fountain, a
boy was filling a plastic bottle with water. A motorist
attempted to park too near the tables and was descended
on by two waiters and the wife of the proprietor, setting
off five minutes of comic opera before he conceded defeat
and drove away.

Nancy ate rapidly, the only sign that she was under any
strain at all. She leaned over her plate and her hair fell

forward, obscuring my view of her face. Who was she? I could not think of her as a friend, let alone my wife. The wine had calmed rather than excited me, and I realized that I meant to keep secret what I knew. To make it a topic of conversation would humiliate me more than I already was. At least I could deprive Nancy of the chance of denying that now she would leave me for Connolly. The future seemed clear. He would apply for laicization —nothing was easier to obtain now—Nancy would divorce me, and they would marry. He would take a familiar route into the lay life, a stolen wife on his arm. Look at Malachi Martin.

"Why don't you ask for the bill?"

"I think I'll sit here a while longer."

She did not quite look at me but hesitated a moment before she nodded and picked up the purse she had propped against her chair. The waiter came forward when she stood, looking inquiringly at me.

"*Ancora un mezzo litro*," I told him.

"*Sì, signore.*"

Nancy stood for a moment with her hand on the back of the chair. "I'm going back."

"Okay."

And that was it. She slung her purse over her shoulder and walked into the street. In a moment she was gone.

I drank several glasses of wine from the second carafe the waiter brought me. But the hostaria no longer seemed quaint, and the Roman street was only a cluster of old buildings. The fountain struck me as an inconvenient and unhygienic way to get water. And it was hot. I paid my bill and went through the deserted streets to the press room, where I wrote a letter of resignation to Gilligan. By telephone I arranged for a flight to New York. I could leave the following morning. What would happen to Nancy? She was no longer my responsibility. Connolly could look after her. Thus it was that I gave her the right to say that I had deserted her.

Sun was already bright at the edges of the drawn plastic shades when the movie ended. Going to meet the sun brought an unreal dawn. My watch read two thirty. Furey raised the shade beside him and looked down at the Atlantic. Over his shoulder he said, "It's been years since I went to Europe by boat."

"That must have been more pleasant than this."

He turned away from the window and sat back in his seat. "I used to go by Holland-America Lines. The *Statendam*."

"I work well on boats."

"I thought you hadn't sailed."

"Not on liners. Freighters."

"What kind of work?"

"Writing."

"What kind of writing?"

"Fiction."

"Mysteries?"

"Not yet."

"I'm looking for someone to write the life of Margaret Rusher."

"Who is she?"

Margaret Rusher had been a Topeka housewife who bore the stigmata and had taken no solid food for over ten years before she died. Furey was convinced she was a saint. I said she reminded me of Theresa Neumann.

"Exactly."

"Is there any thought of canonizing Theresa Neumann?"

He did not know. His interest was Margaret Rusher, about whom he had a great fund of anecdotes. He had apparently visited her often.

"She saw things as they are. She was a woman of incredible clarity although she had little formal education. She predicted the current mess."

"How so?"

"The disloyalty of bishops, priests and nuns deserting their vocations, all of it. She was convinced we are living in the Apocalypse."

If Margaret Rusher was his single candidate for sainthood, he knew of many other mystics and visionaries whose private revelations, invariably of horrendous cataclysms as punishment for sin, raised his hope that his own views would prevail on a cosmic scale. His longing for Armageddon seemed a disguised suicide wish. He rolled toward the window and drew his wallet from his back pocket. From it he took a small medal which he handed me. It looked to be an ordinary cheap miraculous medal.

"Dozens of such medals poured from the hands of Christ on a crucifix owned by Margaret Rusher. Look at it. Where did it come from?"

I handed it back to him. "Extraordinary."

"We are surrounded by the extraordinary."

"I think I'll have a drink."

"I will too."

He wanted rum and Coke. I went forward to the galley for the drinks. Furey was mad. Nancy was mad. In his own way, Connolly had been crazier than both of them. I much preferred being an insignificant hack writer, though my career now seemed in jeopardy. While he drank his rum and Coke, Furey read from a small worn volume the Little Office of the Blessed Virgin. I sipped my bourbon and thought of Maria.

Forty thousand feet above the Atlantic, traveling at hundreds of miles an hour, I was flying back to my child-mistress whose hospitalization was still a mystery to me. The thought that she had had an accident with my car persisted. Would I find her maimed, perhaps unconscious, the dubious benefactor of Italian medicine? The image of her in a hospital bed, swaddled in bandages, disturbed me with its reminder of Gregory. A battered Maria could engage my affection once more. I had missed her beside me in bed. I wanted to hold her again and derive from her youth the strength I needed to keep moving on the exercise wheel my life had become.

Chapter 2

"You look like you've seen a ghost."

Maria squinted up at me from the tousled bed, a tentative smile on her lips. Come from the airport to my apartment, I was startled to find her in my bedroom.

"I thought you were in the hospital."

"Who told you that?"

"Didn't your father come to Rome?"

"He's still here." She sat up in the bed. Only the top button of her pajama jacket was buttoned and her young breasts were visible until she slowly brought the garment closed with a demure hand. Her eyes, noticing what must have been my hungry look, seemed shrewd. "Did you lock the door?" she asked suddenly.

"Yes. Are you expecting your father?"

She shook her head. Austin? I looked around, wondering what had gone on in that bedroom during my absence. But that is all it was, wonder. I had been filled with tenderness at the thought of an injured Maria, but the sight of her whole, spoiled and brassy as ever, addressed little more than my concupiscence. How idiotic I was to have let her move in with me. The trip home, particularly the visit to Newman Hall, put my recent life in a longer perspective, and I did not like what I saw.

"My father doesn't even know about this apartment. He thinks I'm still living up on Monte Mario."

"Where is he staying?"

"The Hilton, where else?"

"His wife said you were in the hospital."

"You talked to her!"

"Just on the phone."

"God." With a disgusted expression on her face, she swung her legs off the bed. "Well, it's my fault. I needed money, and a good way of getting some was to wire him that I had had a recurrence of mono and needed emergency funds for medical treatment." She shook her head, but it was doubtful she really blamed herself. I felt included in her judgment of her father.

"What did you need money for?"

She pursed her lips and widened her eyes, pixielike. Daddy's naughty little girl. "Amalfi."

"I telephoned here several times and got no answer. Did you go to Amalfi?"

"No. My father's response was to hop on a plane and come over. It seemed best to stay up on Monte Mario while he's here."

"But you gave up your room."

"That doesn't mean I can't find a place to sleep."

Again I thought of Austin. It would suit me fine if she

93

went back to him, but I did not like the way she had treated me, my apartment, our plans to go to Amalfi together. It would be easier to let her go if she was mine to let go. Her pajama top had opened again when she sat on the edge of the bed, and it was difficult to ignore the memories evoked by her exposed flesh. She patted the bed beside her and I sat.

"You're tired," she said.

"I want to shower."

She moved closer and I took her in my arms. She put her head against my chest. We might have been father and daughter. "Take your shower while I make us some breakfast."

"It's nearly noon."

"Don't scold." She looked up. Neither love nor desire were in her eyes, only the wish to be coddled and cared for. I kissed her, not as a father kisses his daughter. She pushed me away.

"Go shower. You smell of the United States."

Later, in the bathroom, I wiped the steamy mirror and peered red-eyed at myself. My beard looked like a drowned beast and as I toweled it dry I considered shaving it off. What would Maria say if I emerged clean-shaven from my bath? That was enough to veto the thought. The fear that I would look even older without the beard and lose what small claim I had to Maria kept my hand from the razor. And the fact that the razor was Maria's. I would have needed scissors to get my beard down to the point where I could use a razor on it. It did not seem illogical to me that I should at the same time want to retain and get rid of Maria. Her reaction when I told her of considering shaving surprised me.

"My father has grown a mustache and goatee."

"A new lease on life."

9 4

"He wears blazers and sports coats most of the time too."

"What has he been doing while he's here?"

"Oh, he's made lots of pals at the Hilton. He's seen practically nothing of Rome."

"When does he go back?"

"That's the question. He's having fun. I think I gave him an excuse to get away from what'sherface."

"Will you be seeing him today?"

"He thinks I'm tied up in classes. I have to have dinner with him tonight, though."

"Why did you come back here?"

She held her cup in both hands and looked over its rim at me. "Because I missed you. Jim, why doesn't everybody leave us alone so we can get back to the way it was?"

"Everybody?"

"You know what I mean. You haven't told me anything about your trip."

Years in the fiction trade enabled me to produce an account compatible with her level of interest. Perhaps as I intended she should, she perked up at the mention of Nancy.

"Your ex-wife," she corrected. "Aren't you divorced?"

"Something far more definitive. Our marriage has been declared null and void by Holy Mother Church."

"And you never had any children?"

"No." The last thing I wanted to discuss with Maria was Greg.

Maria stayed with me until after three and then left to go back to Monte Mario and resume her fake student existence for her father's benefit. I straightened the bed and lay down, wanting a nap. Furey and I had shared a cab from the airport and, when I asked to be dropped off on the Corso Vittorio Emanuele, he had repeated his request that I come see him at the Hassler. Lying on my bed, I imagined myself accepting a commission to write the life of Margaret Rusher. The thought led me easily into sleep.

I was wakened with an angry start by a vigorous pounding on my door, and, when I sat up, I realized my head was bursting. It was one of those migraines that come without warning or apparent preamble. I went through the apartment to the front door and looked out the peephole. Whoever was out there stood so close to the door I could see only the fabric of a warm-up jacket. And then he stepped back. It was Austin. Suddenly the pounding began again and I reeled back from the door as if I had been struck, the throbbing in my head assuming the rhythm of his fist on the door. I lowered myself into a chair, trying not to move my head, keeping it level. There are only two ways I know of gaining relief from such headaches. One is to sit perfectly still, preferably in the dark; the other is to hold my breath. In the small center of my mind where thought was possible, it occurred to me that Austin had come to find Maria. My earlier suspicion that the two of them had used my bed returned. Why the hell did he have to pound on the door so hard?

Minutes after his racket stopped, I rose slowly and walked deliberately back to the door. I eased my eye to the hole. He was still out there, a distraught look on his face, his frizzy red hair pulled back in a pony tail. He came forward and I retreated, shutting my eyes against the resumption of his thunderous knocking. But it did not begin. I went back to the bedroom and sat on the edge of the bed, keeping motionless and holding my breath as long as I could. I knew this headache would not leave me until it decided to. With difficulty I rid my mind of the image of the angry hulk of Austin Carey outside my door. If he had come for Maria, why was he so angry? At that moment, with my head pulsing, I would gladly have delivered her over to him. He was right to be enraged that a man as old as I should sleep with the girl he professed to love.

I sat there for half an hour, perhaps longer, and the pain in my head increased. Then, against all experience and better judgment, I decided to go out for some fresh air, for diversion from the ache in my head. I unlocked the door and stepped into the hallway without first having checked the peephole. No matter. Austin Carey had gone away. I took the stairs to the street slowly, balancing my head on my shoulders as if it were a very fragile burden. From the darkened foyer of my building, the bright sunlit street assailed my eyes, and I considered returning to my apartment. But if there was no escaping the pain, going back made no more sense than going on.

I turned left when I came out of the building and had started toward the Campo di Fiori when I heard his voice.

"Clark! Hey, Clark. Wait!"

I turned to see Austin Carey rising from the single table outside the bar across the street. He had trouble getting his long legs free of the small table and in the process tipped over his bottle of beer. It rolled noisily but unbroken toward the center of the narrow street. Pain had mounted when I turned at the sound of his voice. I waited for him as he came toward me.

"I've been looking for you." His face looked as my own had in the steamy mirror after my shower, not quite definite, slightly unreal.

"I've been away."

His smile was contemptuous. "Oh no, you haven't. I've been sitting right here waiting for you."

"To the States. I just got back today."

"I want to talk to you."

I breathed through my mouth, feeling for the first time the nausea that accompanies my headaches. "Talk."

"In private. I mean, sitting down. Not just standing in the street like this."

Across the street an old man had claimed the chair Austin had vacated, opening a used-looking newspaper and getting comfortable in the sun. He would sit there until he was shagged away to make room for a paying customer. The owner of the bar, attracted by the sound of the fallen bottle, came through the strung-bead curtain at the entrance of his bar, glanced at the old man, saw the bottle in the middle of the street, and threw his hands wide in inquiry.

"Pick up the bottle," I said to Austin.

"To hell with the bottle."

"Look, I have a migraine headache. I'm in no mood to talk with you or anyone."

"You're going to be a helluva lot sicker if you don't leave Maria alone."

"How many beers did you have?"

He hit me. It was a tentative blow that struck me in the chest, but it was strong enough to send me staggering backward. The owner of the bar let out a shout of delight, and the old man sat forward over his newspaper, eyes glinting. The mention of Maria as much as Austin's halfhearted blow had caught their attention. A fight over a *ragazza* between a middle-aged man and a college boy promised relief from late afternoon boredom. Austin, to his discredit, was encouraged by the attention. Fists raised, wearing a scowl I might have found comic if my head were not blinding me with pain, Austin advanced on me menacingly.

"Do you want more?"

"Look," I began, and he swung again.

I raised my hands to defend myself and caught this

blow on the arm. Nausea from the migraine swept through me and I doubled over, my eyes afire with pain. I threw up. When I was done, I reached out and supported myself against the door of my building, my legs trembling. But throwing up had purged me somewhat, and my headache was less severe. Perhaps now it would begin to go away. Austin was looking at me with wondrous disgust. The old man raised his newspaper as if to shield himself from my shame. The owner of the bar went to the table and asked the old man what he wanted. With an imperious look, the old man asked for coffee.

Austin said in a loud voice, "If I ever catch you with Maria again I'll beat the shit out of you. I mean that. Don't you have any respect for her at all?"

If this was humiliation, I found it surprisingly easy to bear. The young man with his absurd anger should be ashamed of himself for hitting someone my age. He dropped his hands and, without forethought, I lunged at him, hitting him a glancing blow in the face and then bringing my other fist into his stomach with a rage I seemed to be observing rather than feeling. Austin stumbled backward and I pursued him, flailing away like a madman. He continued to retreat and I to pursue, a pugilistic version of Keats, my fists swinging again and again. I seemed to be lashing out at Nancy and Connolly and every grievance I had been rehearsing during the past ten days. Maybe Maria too was part of my symbolic target. Blood flowed from Austin's nose, and the street filled with onlookers. They seemed to be cheering me on. I think it was that that brought me to my senses.

I stepped back from my victim and was immediately surrounded by well-wishers. The owner of the bar insisted I have a triumphant drink. The old man, risen from his chair, grinned at me like a jack o'lantern. Three nonconsecutive teeth made up his smile.

"Come on, Clark," Austin yelled. "Come on. Don't quit now."

His taunt drew only laughter. I was steered through the beaded curtain into the welcome dimness of the bar. The owner addressed me as Dottore and called his wife to pour me a drink. What would I have? I asked for sweet vermouth and drank it standing at the bar, surrounded by admirers, among them the old man whose coffee was served him there. Around me there circulated various versions of what had happened in the street. It was clear to everyone that I had stolen away the woman of my young assailant and then beaten him soundly when he attacked me. I had become a romantic hero.

The bartender's shirt was open and a green quartz *corno* hung from the golden chain around his neck, moving about on his hairy chest as he beamed up at me. This was the bar where I often had morning coffee, but I had never spoken with the proprietor before. My headache, I realized, was gone. After I finished the vermouth, I pushed through the crowd and went out the beaded curtain into the street. There was no sign of Austin. I turned to the right and went to the Campo di Fiori, crossed it and went up a little street toward the Farnese Palace with the tricolor floating above it. The farther I got from the scene of my ambiguous triumph, the more disgusted with myself I felt. I continued to the river, where, from the embankment, with plane trees casting a mottled shade around me, I looked out at the Tiber. Had Austin been as startled by his violence as I was at mine? The only thing of which I was certain was that Maria had nothing to do with my rage.

When I left the river, I went down the Via Giulia in the direction of the Vatican and took a roundabout way back to my apartment. I approached the building from the direction opposite to the way I had left the bar and slipped in unnoticed. The passage of my headache had left me hungry, but it was too early to go to a restaurant. In my kitchen I made a salami sandwich and ate it with a glass of beer. What in the world was happening to me? I had engaged in a street brawl over a girl of whom I was tired to death.

The Hilton in Rome could have been the Hilton in Corfu or Honolulu or Cleveland or anywhere. Pushing through its doors was like entering Disneyland, where nothing is really real. All about me lay the products of an undemanding imagination. The people too seemed the same you would encounter in Mexico City, Brussels, wherever—not in those cities; in the Hilton hotels in those cities.

These negative thoughts were prompted by the aftermath of my incredible fight with Austin and by what little I knew of Maria's father. Is there anyone so leprously low on the moral thermometer that he does not look condescendingly on those lower still? Who in hell was I to play a minor Dante to these Hiltonians?

I wore a beret and sunglasses and went as swiftly as my feigned limp would allow to a bar off the lobby. Why was I there? To catch a glimpse of Maria with her father. Why? I am not sure. The questions have to end somewhere. Perhaps I needed some vision to force me to make a definitive break with Maria. But, if that was my purpose in coming to the Hilton, I half hoped I would not see them. It was as though I would earn moral credit for trying, no matter the outcome. The point of it all was punitive and penitential. In the bar I sat in the deeper gloom at a small table and ordered a gin and tonic from the half-clad waitress. Given Maria's propensity for drink, the bar seemed as good a place as any to catch a glimpse of father and daughter together. The lobby was too public. My disguise would not deceive Maria there. My presence as well as my identity could go unperceived in the bar.

Gin and tonic. The setting seemed to call out for that drink. To order it seemed an assertion of spring. I had scarcely started on it when I saw Maria through the entrance of the bar. She was loitering with a man before the display cases of a boutique at which residents of the hotel could pay several times as much for items as they would in the city. Would they come into the bar? I watched them as well as I could through the intervening traffic of the guests. Then they were gone. I waited where I was, but they did not come into the bar. I rose from my table.

The impression I had received of him from the bar had not been wrong. Maria's father looked younger than I did, younger than anyone my age. Maria was twenty, her father should be forty at the very least unless he had married in puberty. I began to limp more exaggeratedly as I followed them at a distance. And then Maria turned and saw me. Her mouth opened in surprise, and then she burst into laughter. Her father was shocked at the spectacle of his daughter laughing at a lame man. I continued toward them, mesmerized, caught by my curiosity.

"Where in the world did you get that outfit?" Maria burbled when I reached them.

Her father, smiling nervously, looked at me. Since I was still wearing sunglasses, he must have seen reflections of himself.

"Daddy, this is Jim Clark. He's an American writer who lives in Rome."

This description of me seemed to reassure her father, explaining the beret, the beard, the glasses, perhaps the limp as well. He extended his hand.

"Dave Miller."

I shook his hand. He looked no older close up; the mustache and goatee had a barbered look, enhancing his youthfulness. I told myself he led a pampered life, that he would belong to health clubs, perhaps jog along the lakefront every morning, working up a salvific sweat.

"You live here permanently, Mr. Clark?"

"Jim. Nothing's permanent. I've lived here a number of years." When Miller looked around the lobby as if at the setting of my life, I added, "In the central city."

"The inner city?"

He seemed to be trying to place me in the categories that governed his thought. The phrase suggested buildings ready for the wrecking ball. Doubtless an American bureaucrat would see the buildings of old Rome as ripe for urban renewal. Il Duce had had similar ideas, but he had acted on them between Rome and the sea, creating EUR from scratch.

"Our only hesitation about Maria's coming here concerned where she would live."

"I'm told the student accommodations are very nice."

"The security is good. I checked on that."

"I was having a drink in the bar when I saw you go by."

"Would you have a drink with us?"

Maria looked dubious. I removed my sunglasses and winked at her behind her father's back. Now she looked alarmed.

"How did Maria come to know you?" Miller asked when we were settled in the gloom. Above us, from a spot sunk in the ceiling, weak light descended as in a Pentecost by a lesser Renaissance artist.

"Through a young man, her boyfriend, I believe. Austin Carey." I faced Maria. "I just ran into him near the Campo di Fiori."

"Is he a student?" The question was paternal, interested.

"About as much as I am."

"What do you mean?"

"He's not too smart."

Miller turned and his features caught the overhead spot. "You have enormous amounts of talent. All you need is motivation."

"They don't teach that here."

"It can be learned, you know. There are motivation seminars."

I asked about these, curious, and he was happy to speak of them, perhaps wanting to get away from Maria's low estimate of herself. In one such seminar, after the participants were settled, they were told to get up and look under their chairs. Each found a dollar bill taped there. The message? In order to make a buck you've got to get up off your ass.

"Do such sessions really work?"

"No doubt about it. I've attended myself and sent young men to them. They never fail. Half of life is psychological."

"At least," I agreed.

Miller smiled with complicity. "Right. Probably a helluva lot more, if we really knew."

"Are these seminars aimed only at businessmen?"

"The ones I've attended, yes. But the concept is universal. It can be applied to anything."

"To students?" I asked.

"Maybe even to writers." There was a warning note in Maria's voice. She clearly thought this shared drink unwise; but then she had not been consulted.

"Would I have read anything of yours?" Miller asked.

"Do you read science fiction?"

"I'm afraid not. Do you also teach?"

"You're interested in learning to write?"

"No." He laughed. Maria tipped her head to one side and looked warningly at me. "I meant at Loyola. Are you on the staff there?"

Did he think I might be the professor with whom Maria had had an affair in Chicago?

"I talk to the students, but not on a regular basis. I did mention I ran into Austin, didn't I, Maria?"

Miller said, "Maria scared the hell out of me. That's why I'm here. Did you hear about it?"

"I just got back from the States this morning."

"She sent a wire that sounded as though she were dying. Why can't they just say they need money?"

"Okay," Maria said. "I'll say it. I need money for travel, a trip to the Amalfi coast, one to Greece, maybe another to Israel."

"You're here to study, not travel."

"Travel is a kind of study."

He liked that. "Yes, I suppose it is. It always expands my horizons to go to a foreign country." He looked around the American bar as Stanley might have looked at darkest Africa.

"The Amalfi coast is beautiful," I said. "Have you been there?"

"No, I haven't."

"It's in southern Italy," Maria said, and he gave her a cold look. Daughter or not, she could not treat him as if he were an ass.

He said, "I'm glad they haven't moved it."

One of the oddities of the half hour I spent with Maria and her father was that sometimes I felt allied with her against him while at other times, as when he made that retort about Amalfi, I felt that Miller and I must put down his smart-ass daughter.

"Look," he said. "What are you doing for dinner? Maria and I are going down into Rome tonight, and you're welcome to join us."

"I wish I could. Thank you very much. Perhaps another time. How long are you staying?"

"I return tomorrow. This is my last fling."

"When you come back, then."

"I threw a coin in that fountain."

Maria winced, but he did not see it, luckily for her, I thought. I could imagine Maria's mother treating Miller with condescension, her tone apologizing for what he said and did and was. On balance I liked him, with his well-groomed face hair, red plaid sport coat and knowledge-ability about motivation seminars. He wanted to go back to his room before leaving the hotel, so Maria and I had a few minutes together.

"What a sneaky thing to do, coming here."

"I was in the neighborhood."

"Sure. What was all that about Austin?"

"He woke me up, pounding on the door. He was lying in wait for me in the street."

"My God. What happened?"

"We fought."

"Did he hurt you? No wonder you're wearing sun-glasses. Let me see."

"Actually I beat him. It was quite a triumph. Throngs of cheering partisans, afterward a hero's drink, very satisfying."

"You had a fight with Austin in the street!"

"That's right. After he attacked me."

"Jim, he'll never forget that. He'll kill you. He's been under the care of psychiatrists most of his life. I've never known anyone so spacey. I mean, he looks like a football player and all that, but he isn't, not inside. He's more or less of a complete mess. He remembers things you said, weeks ago, months ago, and you realize he's been brood-ing about them all the time."

"Things I've said?"

"What anybody says."

"Like you."

"Yes. He wants to know what I really meant when I said something I don't even remember saying. Weird. And he's violent."

"I found that out." But I felt I was finding out about Maria and Austin too. "I'm violent too, apparently."

"I wish you hadn't fought with him."

"So do I."

"What do you think of my father?"

"I like him."

"He's not stupid. He's really very bright. Shrewd. He's rich."

"I believe it. I didn't think him at all stupid. Of course he did marry again."

"So?"

"He doesn't learn from his mistakes."

She stuck out her tongue at me.

The following morning I sat down to my typewriter, rolled a piece of paper into it, and realized that I had nothing to write. My exchange with Cassell had undermined the habitual confidence with which I sail into gripping tales for boys. If the demand for my product was disappearing, the long effort of even a short book was a luxury I could not afford. I sat there fashioning refutations of Cassell's remarks, but, after all, he was the one who knew the market. There was no doubt that, by following his advice, I had done well for a number of years. How could I now just set aside his judgment of my typical work?

As for the "realistic" juveniles he suggested I try, I did not have the heart for them. I did not write fiction to enable my reader to adjust to the world. On that score, I was in agreement with Evelyn Waugh's Scott-King, who thought it wicked to do anything to fit a boy for the modern world. My forte was escape, adventure, the heightened unreal world where a reader's dreams are encouraged.

Mysteries? I typed a note to myself in which I set down what little I knew of the genre and could find in what I wrote no recipe for going on. No day's stint suggested itself, though the mystery novel as genre appealed to me. The mystery writer enters into a pact with a reader who wants to be deceived, but fairly. I imagined unexplained corpses lying about in odd places and murders effected by means more terrible for being items of everyday life. The lethal salt cellar, torture by lawn mower, the hair dryer dropped into the tub while the victim soaks away his troubles, the car left running in the garage.

Gimmicks, and all of them too abstract; no story formed. For two days I tried unsuccessfully to get started on a mystery novel, refusing to answer the phone. Once there came a tapping on my door and I looked through the peephole, half fearing it was Austin Carey, but it was Maria.

"I can't stay," she said, when I had let her in. "Why don't you answer your phone?"

"I'm in the throes of composition." How I wished that were true.

"Has Austin been back here?"

"Not that I know of."

"Jim, I'm frightened. He told me very calmly that he would get even with you."

"Are you staying with him?"

Her look was reproachful. "I am trying to keep him away from you."

I should have been grateful, I suppose, but my fight with Austin made it difficult for me to share her fears. And my fruitless hours at the typewriter were not good for my self-esteem. Now Maria presented herself as my protectress.

1 0 8

"I'll stop answering the door."

"Don't be a shit."

"I'm sorry."

And I was. Her presence seemed to drive defeat from the room, and my real fears that I would no longer be able to support myself by writing. But when I attempted to take her into my arms she resisted.

"I've got to go. He mustn't know I've been here."

"Give him my love."

"You are a shit."

But tenderness mixed with the anger in her voice. She kissed me, went to the door and stopped. "God, I'd like to stay."

"I wish you would."

We stood looking at one another. It no longer seemed absurd to me that I should love her. Did I love her? I wanted her, certainly. She shook her head.

"We'll make up for it. Later."

After she had gone, I locked the door again and went back to my typewriter, but my attempts to write a mystery went even more badly after Maria's visit. Finally I decided to go down to the Hassler and see Furey.

"You should have called first," he said. "I haven't much time right now."

"I decided to come on the spur of the moment." I wanted to keep my visit casual in appearance. Furey must not be allowed to suspect the desperation with which I came to his suite.

"Have you been considering my proposition about the life of Margaret Rusher?"

"I'd like to hear it again."

"What do you know about her?"

"Except what you told me on the plane, nothing. It's not my sort of thing. Do you know the kind of thing I write?"

"I do now. I had someone look into it for me. Your agent Cassell is receptive to the idea of a commissioned work."

"Perhaps he'd like to write it."

Furey puffed on his cigarette. "I want as factual a presentation of her life as possible. Nothing saccharine. The simple truth. Gilligan seems to think you've lost your faith." He waved aside what I was about to say. "Even if he overstated it, a healthy skepticism could be a plus. Pious pliable writers are a dime a dozen. That isn't what I want. I would like to see someone try to explain away the facts of her life. When that proves impossible, the story will be more persuasive."

"I couldn't do it."

"Then why did you come see me?"

"I don't know."

"I do. Your career is in jeopardy. I made a very thorough check. You have been remarkably successful writing adventure stories, good wholesome stories, too, I'm told, but your style is no longer wanted. You need a job, Clark." He said it matter-of-factly, with the practiced ease of one used to having the advantage over others. "I have an alternative to Margaret Rusher I think you will like. I thought of it first on the plane. You knew Michael Connolly. How would you like to write a book about him?"

The doors to the balcony were open, and billowing curtains advanced ghostlike into the room and then withdrew as they ran out of breeze. From below came the sounds of the Via Sistina. I found myself smiling. I had half a notion to tell Furey that Connolly had been seen since his burial. It was the kind of tidbit the old man would like, though not perhaps about someone like Michael Connolly. His alternative suggestion might not be so different from his first as he supposed. I shook my head.

"I don't think so."

"I want you to think about it. I am prepared to advance you twenty thousand dollars. Cassell regards that as fair."

"You've discussed this with him?"

"It's all I discussed with him. I didn't think you would want to write Margaret Rusher's biography. Connolly is a different matter."

"He was a friend of mine." I thought I detected a Judas note in my voice.

"I realize that. I consider it an advantage."

"You'd never make your investment back on a book about Connolly."

"Who knows? It would be worth the money if you could explain to me what made that man tick."

Furey stood, a tall old man in a rumpled suit. Unlikely as he looked, he fitted in at the Hassler. Perhaps it was his seigneurial manner. I admired his brass, attempting to buy me first one way and then another. Was he doing this as a favor to Gilligan? The best thing he could do for his old friend would be to subsidize *Alleluia*. He came with me to the door.

"I will be here for at least a week more. Give me your answer in the next five days."

"You seriously want to commission a life of Michael Connolly?"

"I consider twenty thousand dollars serious."

I left without saying no again, and I did not like myself for rising to his bait. My problem was that I did not have a great number of choices. Downstairs the doorman let me push through into the street unaided. He knew a Hassler type when he saw one.

When I came onto the walk outside, I ran into Milly Wilson and was caught up in the kind of public hugging and kissing that embarrasses me.

"Jimmy, we were talking about you only the other day."

The great lenses of her sunglasses grew less opaque in the shadow of the hotel. "Ian worries about you living in the *centro*. Have you been robbed yet?"

"No, but I was attacked on the street outside my apartment."

She let out a squeal, whether of shock or delight at having her fears confirmed I could not tell.

"Were you harmed?" She swept off her sunglasses in a grand gesture and peered at me through heavily made-up eyes. Milly was brown as a berry and looked in wonderful shape.

"I got the better of him. Or so the spectators told me."

"You fought with your attacker!" She turned her head slightly to one side. Naughty, naughty. "He will be back with others like himself."

"Like the exorcised devils?"

She did not catch the allusion, but a disconnected comprehension shone in her large green-and-silver-painted eyes. "Have you moved to the Hassler?"

"Milly, I couldn't afford that."

"What are you doing for lunch?"

"Eating."

She frowned patiently. "Alone?"

"Surely you're not."

She had not intended to lunch at all. She had come into town to buy a few things and thought she'd pop into the Hassler for tea. We went down to Alla Rampa where Milly demanded and got an outside table, the waiter bringing out another from inside and wedging it among those already there. Her manner would have been difficult for even a Roman to ignore. She did not tip the headwaiter or even acknowledge that a favor had been done us. Her back was to the waiter when he made a gesture summing the matter up.

"Jimmy, I do wish you'd live in a more sensible place.

Ian and I would never forgive ourselves if something happened to you. How is Nancy?"

"I saw her a few days ago."

"Is she in Italy?"

"I was in the States. I don't suppose you remember a man named Connolly? A priest. An American. No? Well, why should you? He was a friend of ours. He was in that plane crash in Washington. I went home for the funeral and saw Nancy."

"Tell me all about her."

What an awful lot there seemed to say, but as I spoke I kept remembering the one thing I could never tell Milly: Nancy's claim to having seen the dead man. Milly was full of curiosity about Nancy's apartment, its exact location in Washington, and the life she now led. The account I gave of our lunch in Georgetown brought a sentimental smile to Milly's face.

"You two were meant for each other, Jimmy. It is so sad that you should have parted."

"Nancy was granted an annulment."

"I will never understand the Roman Church."

Ian and Milly were Anglicans of the more or less cultural sort. From time to time they attended services at St. Paul's on Via Nazionale, and Milly put in an afternoon a month with Oxfam.

"No one ever has."

"I thought nonconsummation was the only grounds."

"There have always been others. But times have changed. Everything is psychology now. Did one truly have the intention to enter into marriage? That sort of thing."

"Are you going to call that waiter, or must I die of thirst right here in the open air?" She had finished her gin and tonic and wanted another.

Milly had been Nancy's friend. They'd met at an ecumenical do held at Santa Susanna years ago, and we had come to know her and Ian well. It was the Wilsons to whom Nancy turned when I left abruptly for home. Since returning to Rome alone, I had seen them infrequently. Our conversations turned too much on what was no more to be entirely comfortable for me. Ian had an odd enthusiasm for my books—they were among the few friends who knew what books I wrote—and that was flattering. Besides, they were well off and generous, and it was always a treat to be entertained at their apartment in Parioli or, better, at their country place near Tivoli. Since Maria had moved in with me, I had avoided the Wilsons, several times turning down invitations. As often as not, there was an unattached female at the parties they invited me to, and I did not want them to learn how I had arranged that side of my life.

Lunching with Milly at the Ristorante Alla Rampa, chattering about Nancy, I was conscious of how much I did want to tell her—about Maria, about the perilous state of my writing career. Although I had gone to Furey, I could not admit to myself that fiction was now closed to me. What I needed was peace and quiet, an extended period during which I could start off in a new direction. Yet I had not turned down Furey's surprising suggestion that I write a book about Michael Connolly. The one thing I would not do was the realistic juveniles Cassell had spoken of. Scott-King does not compromise.

"Does Nancy ever speak of coming for a visit?"

"Not to me. Her memories of Rome are not all that pleasant. Apart from the friends we made here, of course."

"She always struck me as a little jealous. Did I ever tell you that? When the four of us were together, she kept such a close watch on you."

"That must have been your imagination."

"A woman doesn't imagine things like that. Of course Ian was quite taken by her. All that American openness has such a devastating effect on him. I suppose he thought they could be pals at least. Is she thinking of remarrying?"

What strangers Nancy and I seemed in Milly's version of us. Whenever Milly lifted a glass or fork, half a dozen bracelets slid down her slim wrist, and she had a way of leaning toward me when she spoke that suggested she was offering herself, the glimpse thus given of her golden body a promissory note. It was all pretense, of course. Milly would never give Ian the least excuse for suspecting her, something he would certainly do if she ever stopped her inconsequential flirtatiousness. Her green velvety dress made her auburn hair look redder than it was. She was undeniably a handsome woman. Years ago a Pan Am executive, resident in Rome, had acted on the invitation she seemed to issue, and there had been shocked reaction on Milly's part. Even if I had not known that, I was in the grips of such a longing for abstinence I would have been immune to her charms. I assured Milly that Nancy gave no indication of wanting to marry again.

"How I'd love to see her."

"Aren't you due for a trip to the States?"

"I wish I were. But we're off to England next week for nearly a month. Ian's family." She made a face. "The three of us must absolutely get together before we leave."

So we arranged to have dinner the following night, at George's, Ian's treat, and it was a treat of another kind to feign reluctance when, over brandy, the two of them began to insist that I must withdraw to their country place, away from the violence of Rome. Austin's attack had convinced the Wilsons I was living in mortal danger. They were as nervous as Maria.

"You should never fight back, for God's sake. Give

them money and count it well spent. Whoever thought these things would come to Italy? When we first came here, Rome was a city where one was safe on the streets at any hour of the day or night. I can understand it when politicians are targets, James." Ian held his brandy under his nose and inhaled. "Politicians deserve everything they get, particularly Italian politicians. But it has become indiscriminate. It is as bad as New York."

"Ian, I spend most of my day behind locked doors writing. I'm on a special project."

That afternoon I had telephoned Furey and told him his idea of a book on Michael Connolly had caught my imagination. He did not sound surprised. The money would be deposited to my account in the Banca d'America e d'Italia. With that as security, I hoped I could learn the art of mystery novel writing and, eventually, return Furey's money. This was disingenuous, but I was really worried.

"In the country you can write indoors, outdoors, anywhere you like. You could have weeks without interruption. Do you remember the place at all?"

"Ian has made so many improvements since you were last there," Milly said. "A pool, tennis courts. Of course the abbey has just gobbled up money. You won't recognize the place."

"Total isolation," Ian said emphatically.

"Jimmy saw Nancy in Washington when he was over there."

"Cable her," Ian said. "She can stay with you. There's loads of room."

Milly gave him a look and, remembering, he dropped that line, but after all, it was she who had brought up Nancy.

It was in a dreary nightclub off the Via Veneto with flashing lights and near-nude dancers writhing to the thunderous beat of the music that I accepted Ian's offer of the gate house at his country home as a place where I might write during the coming weeks.

"I'll take you up tomorrow and show you around. Did Milly tell you of our trip to England?"

So it was settled. Like Horace, I would withdraw to Ian's equivalent of the Sabine farm. And, like the pagan poet, I would do so with a sense of escaping Rome.

Chapter 3

In the morning cocks crowed near and far, and from across the valley came the precise intonation of a church bell announcing that a priest was saying his Mass, and saying it very early indeed. I noticed this with satisfaction, still in bed, sleep in my eyes, the fresh mountain air a tonic to my lungs. The smoking I had resumed on a whim the day I learned of Connolly's death had become a habit once more. Perhaps a further bonus of my stay at the Wilsons' country place would be to free me from it. Yet the thought had lost the urgency it had once had. I could look back on years of not smoking and doubt they had gained me a longevity not already determined by my genes. Connolly had quit smoking before I had, and Connolly was dead.

If I overslept that priest, I did rise early in the country. My bedroom windows opened onto a balcony from which, looking westward, I watched the hills receive the light of the rising sun. Standing there with a cup of tea in one hand and a cigarette in the other, I felt returned to the Italy that had charmed me when Nancy and I first came here years before. My eye was drawn to the far horizon, but just below me and to the right, built on a plateau, was the stone farmhouse the Wilsons had remodeled into their country place. The first level, once the dwelling of cows and sheep, had been reclaimed, the huge living room making artful use of the brick supporting arches that had once marked the limits of the stalls. The fireplace there was manorial, a "walk-in," Ian Wilson termed it.

There had been a peasant family resident in an apartment at one end of the main house, but they were gone now. Ian had told me the story the day we drove up together.

"Did I tell you how I lost my peasants, Jim?"

He made it sound as if he had a runaway-slave problem. The family, just a couple, no children, had looked after the main house, the woman cooking and cleaning, the man cultivating the vines, keeping fences in repair and tending to the many innovations Ian had introduced, among them the swimming pool. The man had been unable to master the filter. Ian would arrive, ready to plunge into his pool, only to find its surface alive with strange growths, leaves and branches afloat on it, unusable. What could he do but take out his wrath on his alleged caretaker? In the taverna of the village above the farm, in his cups with other Communists who resented foreigners like Ian buying up their countryside, the peasant had whipped up his courage and, prodded by his drinking comrades, resolved to quit. This brought on a terrible fight with his wife, who knew they would never find another sinecure like this. Hers had become a life of comparative ease. Except for weekends, when the Wilsons filled their house with guests and there was much cooking and cleaning to do, her days were blissfully her own. The prospect of returning to marginal farming at the exorbitant rents now charged for land was not her notion of liberation, nor did her husband's garbled account of how spitting in the Englishman's face would advance the revolution persuade her. They already had what the mutterers in the taverna hoped for in some vague tomorrow. The upshot was that she was stabbed and then abandoned by her distraught and remorseful husband. She crawled up the hill to the village, where she arrived half dead from loss of blood. She now languished in a hospital, and the husband, cut down from the beam in a barn where he had attempted suicide, awaited trial in the little jail of Civitella di Licenza.

"You can imagine what drunken vendettas were hatched in the taverna, James. There were incidents. Some broken windows and machinery, shit in the pool, slogans painted in red across a fence. And the boulder. The boulder could have been a very bad thing."

"The boulder," I said.

"Of course I told Milly it was accidental." After all these years in their country, Ian drove like the Italians, and I was eager to be distracted from the perils of the road.

"Tell me about it."

"My dear fellow, this huge boulder came rolling down the hill at the foot of which we live, bounded across the terrace just off the sitting room, scaring, I don't mind telling you, the piss out of yours truly."

Why hadn't he mentioned these things last night? "How long ago did that happen?"

Ian put a thoughtful finger on his chin. With a sharp twist of his other hand he got us out of the path of a truck that was bearing down upon us. "More than a month ago," he decided and got both hands back on the steering wheel.

"Am I to be a guest or a target up there?"

"Have no fear, Jim. Everything has been settled through the priest. I have become a benefactor of the church. Not that I was ever afraid. I acted for Milly's sake. These people may stab a wife in a fit of drunken anger, but they will not confront an adversary. Think of their African campaigns. The truth is, they are cowards, by and large."

There were intimations of the old colonial hand in Ian's tone. But then he had lived outside England all his life, save for some years of schooling. He had been a tobacco broker in Italy for more than twenty years. He loved the country and had genuine affection for the natives, but there was something of condescension in his attitude toward them. He was dealing with wogs, after all, and wogs simply are not British. We Americans will never master the air of easy superiority that enabled a small island to end up as custodian of a very large fraction of the earth.

"I wish you had told me all this before."

He looked at me tolerantly and his eyes dropped to the book I held so tightly my knuckles were discolored. "What are you reading?"

"Cicero."

"Didn't he live up by my place?"

"That was Horace."

Ian's wild driving did not allow me the pleasure I had anticipated from this trip into the Castelli Romani, past

Hadrian's villa and on up into Tivoli. I began to talk nervously.

"You should read Gilbert Highet's *Poets in a Landscape*, Ian. Chapters in it amount to a guidebook of this region. There is quite an extensive discussion of Horace. Did you know that Trollope wrote a book on Horace?" Ian did not know. "Not many people do. He was prouder of it than of his novels. Of course I can't agree with him on that. Alfred Noyes did too."

"Did what?"

"Wrote a book on Horace."

It was the kind of talk Connolly and I had engaged in on the road at Newman Hall. I mention this babble because it is half the explanation for not changing my mind about staying in the Wilsons' country place. The proximity of Horace's villa touched memories that went back to the shores of Lake Jemima, where I had read, besides Horace himself, the books I mentioned to Ian. I translated several of the odes into English verse and published them in the school paper, and that has always given me a proprietary feeling for the Roman poet. He became mine in a special way, and I have gone back to him over the years, reading the same Bennett and Rolfe edition I used in a basement classroom at Newman Hall. Catullus had been momentary fun, but Horace was a lasting pleasure.

The second part of the explanation was the sight of the ruined abbey on the Wilson property. Ian, with a flair for the dramatic, brought the car around a turn in the road and stopped so that we were overlooking his farm and had a view of the landscape dropping away toward Rome and, beyond, to the sea. My eyes were solely for the remnants of medieval walls, which stood on a grassy promontory beyond the farmhouse that had been built of stones taken from it. The tower alone had survived intact, its squat square claim on those coordinates of space reposing on eight centuries of presence. Seeing it again after a lapse of years, and just returned from my trip to Wisconsin, I linked the tower of the ruined abbey with the tower of Newman Hall. Somehow the defiant survival of the monastery tower seemed recompense for what had happened to my old school. Take the long view. That might have been Italy's message to me. Things take their quiet revenge on the men who wrong them.

Ian put the car back in gear, went through the gate and down a graveled drive to the house, not even alluding to the guest house as we went by. We got out of the car, went round the house and crossed the lawn to the stone steps leading up to the abbey.

"We've had archaeological teams here twice. They wrote it up. I'll show you the articles. This medieval stuff will appeal to a Catholic like yourself."

I did not bother to correct him. Ian had obviously gone to great expense to prevent the further deterioration of the abbey. The walls of the tower had been reinforced, the cloister walk freed of covering earth, the crypt restored.

"Several graves down there. They buried their dead all over the place. Bones kept cropping up. Come here."

Where we stood had been the main floor of the abbey church. At one end a partial wall contained the arched outline of the doors. The floor itself, for years covered with silt, was powerfully evocative of sandaled feet, the passage of monks, another time. Ian crouched next to a large sheet of plywood from which he had removed the anchoring stone. He lifted the plywood and beckoned me to look. Below was a portion of the crypt that had been sealed off in the restoration efforts to form a small room.

"Can you see those plastic bags?"

I could not make out anything clearly until Ian moved and sunlight entered the underground room. Plastic shimmered in the sun, a twentieth-century artifact hidden away in the ruins of the eleventh.

"Those are bones collected from around the place as they dug. The priest up above came and we had a little ceremony, a sort of reburial. I gave the priest a good stipend. Nice little crowd. Wine afterward. A great success. That pretty well put the bad business behind us. Haven't had any trouble since."

My eyes were fixed on the plastic bags containing the bones of men who had lived only God knew how many centuries ago, men dedicated to God in a regulated life determined by their vows. Poverty, chastity, obedience. I turned and looked out across the valley at the contours of the land. Had the view altered much since the men whose bones those were looked down the valley in the direction of Rome?

"A bit ghoulish, I suppose." Ian dropped the plywood over the opening and moved the rock back on top of it with the toe of his loafer.

Ghoulish? What I felt was that I would not be entirely alone here, not with all the departed in their plastic bags. The thought of the dead Michael Connolly drifted across my mind, but I let it go.

We retraced our steps. Lawn surrounded the house on three sides, a very English-looking lawn. On the south side was the swimming pool, now only a molded concrete basin perhaps twenty yards long. Ian and I walked to the terrace at the north end of the house. It was across this terrace that a boulder had rolled after coming down the hill that loomed above.

"I left the bugger where it stopped." Ian pointed. "It sailed right across the lawn and was only slowed and stopped by the rise up to the abbey."

The boulder was large enough, certainly, but somehow it did not seem a serious object. I looked up at Civitella di Licenza. A very steep ascent. A wall was visible and the steeple of the church, but the rest from where we stood was lost in a cloud of trees. Ian took me on to his tennis courts and vineyards, then, and we ended back on the terrace having a glass of Ian's own wine.

Any misgivings I had felt on the ride up had long since disappeared. The sight of the place convinced me that here I would be able to write my way out of the impasse I was in.

I moved into the guest house the following day. This house, built on the steep incline, had three levels with a room on each one. The lowest was the kitchen, modern as could be. A bedroom with adjoining bath was at the highest level: raftered ceiling, plaster walls, windows that opened onto a balcony. The room between these two became my study. I set up shop on a refectory table Ian had helped me move close to the windows. Seated at it, I could look out at the abbey. It was there, where solemn thoughts seemed mandatory, that I returned to the frivolous task of telling imaginary tales. The cat that came with the guest house was a sleek, slinking mute whose wide-eyed watching seemed to chide me. Country sounds came to me on the April air—the bleat of a lamb, the lowing of cattle, dogs barking—while I tried to write of an apparently insoluble murder in faraway America. A man stages his own death and arranges clues so that his wife will be suspected. I wrote it from her point of view and was aiming at an easy irony. The man would be murdered in the end, caught in the web he had elaborately constructed to catch his wife.

I wrote regularly but not in haste, establishing my customary routine, five pages every morning. The click that tells me I am on my way refused to come, but I added doggedly to my pages. The reward for work was to wander about the place afterward, and it was the ruined abbey that fascinated me.

The archaeological reports Ian had mentioned were published by the British School in Rome. One was a very technical account illustrated with photographs in which meter sticks were laid alongside objects to establish their size. For several days that article was my guide as I wandered about the ruins. The other study was historical. In the course of its existence the monastery had been occupied by a succession of religious orders: Benedictines at first, then several lesser orders, finally the Celestini, so-called because of the sky-blue habits they wore. The cloister walk went round a rectangle enclosing a well. It was still a good well. Ian had installed an electric pump and used the well to water the grass and other greenery he had planted in the ruins. There was a fading mural on the remains of the refectory wall. What seemed to be Christ looked down at me, and I imagined men centuries dead lifting their eyes to that same painting.

I would often end up by that sheet of plywood Ian had lifted to display the plastic bags of bones. No matter how often I lifted the cover to look down at them, I continued to feel an eerie tremor. I developed the fantasy that I had entered the religious life, become a monk in a defunct community, my cloister open to the skies. Bare ruined choirs where late the sweet birds sang . . .

The cat followed me around like a familiar, noiselessly inquisitive. Sometimes I would turn to find him there and start with surprise. But mainly I wrote and read, welcoming the return of routine to my days, the rhythm of work and rest, the steady accumulation of pages beside my typewriter. It was difficult to tell whether the mystery I was writing was any good, and from time to time I would feel guilty about the money I had taken from Furey to underwrite my venture into a new fictional genre.

There were times when I missed Maria and the lengthy excursion out of character my living with her represented —or so, at least, I tried to describe it to myself. The ghosts of celibates were in the air, and I was a little ashamed of the extended carnal interlude I had passed with Maria. How easily we imagine the deeds we do have nothing to do with the person we are. Among the ghosts that haunted me was that of my dead son. I imagined him aware of his father, watching me from afar, saddened by the person I had become. It was tempting to enter into a pact with his memory and pledge myself to ascetic heroism, a monkish life of abnegation. I cut down on cigarettes a bit, I drank only a little wine at meals, I worked.

And finally I became bored. It seemed time to take a break. I decided to drive down to Rome and check my mail.

Chapter 4

My *portiere* handed me my mail and, without removing the cigarette from his mouth, took the thousand-lira note I gave him. When he thanked me, the cigarette's bobbing would have made reading his lips difficult. On the street outside, traffic had been stopped by an oversize truck whose driver seemed reluctant to admit that he could not squeeze his vehicle down the narrow thoroughfare. The noxious smell of exhaust invaded the entryway of my building. It surprised me that the *portiere*, who considered that street his turf, had not gone out to adjudicate matters.

"*Fa caldo,*" I said, but he did not hear me.

I hesitated because, having picked up my mail, I did not know if I wanted to go upstairs to my apartment. It was after one o'clock and I was hungry. The *portiere* came out of his little cubicle and seemed to notice the chaos in the street for the first time. He buttoned his uniformlike coat, squared his shoulders and sauntered out the door and into battle. I followed him out but went to where I had parked my car on the Corso Vittorio Emanuele.

In Trastevere I bought some newspapers and strolled down a little street to the Piazza di Santa Maria. Sabatini's was crowded so I continued to a trattoria where I sat at an outside table and ordered insalata mista, melanzane and a *mezzo* of red.

"Acqua minerale?" The waiter was young and his look was sly. No doubt he had been coached in the art of urging tourists into extravagance.

"*Un mezzo*," I said and, as he turned away, called after him, "*Non gazzata.*"

The trattoria tables were enclosed by tubs of flowers set in metal stands and, in a patch of sun, a cat slept on the cobbles. I thought of my feline companion at the Abbadia Celestina. My waiter brought a basket of bread, water and wine. It was almost liturgical.

As I took my first taste of the wine a young man stopped at the entrance to the eating area and spoke with one of the waiters. He received a nod and took a mandolin from a gray cloth bag and began to play, very delicately and with an expression of compromised integrity. His coat was gabardine, and he wore nonmatching trousers and a dark turtleneck sweater. I could not open mail or read a paper while he played. Here was an artist more humble than myself. Who was I to deny him my attention? After he had played for ten minutes, he passed among the tables, accepting offerings with an averted face. I wondered what youthful dreams of glory had degenerated to this. He put his mandolin back into its sack, picked up a brief case he had leaned against a table leg, and went off down the street, to another trattoria, perhaps even to Sabatini's. On what modest scale did he now measure his success?

Hardly had the mandolin player gone out of sight when another musician came along, less dignified than the first, carrying his instrument in a case. He opened this outside the trattoria enclosure, assembled a clarinet and began to toot away. The sleeping cat was as undisturbed by this as he had been by the mandolin. A couple at a table placed against the outer wall of the building were a better audience.

The man was middle-aged, the woman very young. His daughter? More likely his mistress, an inexpensive meal in Trastevere prelude to the rest of the afternoon in bed. The man's mouth was greasy with food and he drank wine with thirsty intemperance. He repelled me as, I suppose, I repelled Austin. What superiority could I claim to that aging lover bringing a forkful of chicken to his greedy mouth? The fact that I was now willing to end the affair did not really alter matters. The future does not undo the past. In Austin's shoes I would have, perhaps, the same murderous thoughts. When my food came I picked at it fastidiously, trying to summon an ascetic disregard for carnal pleasures. My little pile of letters waited like dessert to stir my jaded appetite.

Besides the inevitable bills, there were letters from Nancy and Cassell. Postponed gratification seemed an affectation, and I began to open envelopes with my table knife. Statements from several credit card companies proved to be a surprise. It seemed far too soon for my air fare from Chicago to appear on a statement, but what startled me was an entry indicating a charge to the Kunert Shipping Lines. I had often sailed on Kunert in the past, but this charge made no sense. A number of other entries on other accounts were equally puzzling. I decided that so many errors were better than one. One I might have overlooked. In the age of the computer, larceny comes in several sizes still. I could not attribute malice to the machine itself. Nonetheless, the errors were an annoyance, promising hours of complaint before the items were removed from my statement.

Nancy's letter was more of a surprise. The news that I had been commissioned to write the life of Michael Connolly stirred her to real anger.

If I could believe that you meant to put him before the public as he really was I could perhaps forgive this exploitation of his memory, but your way of talking about him when you were here, to say nothing of old grievances I above all know you have, suggests that you have in mind something other than a favorable presentation. You would not listen to me your last night here, and I question your right to write his life when it is very likely premature that this should be done. Jim, he was here. He came to see me and we talked and what he had to say was nothing short of amazing. I would not hesitate to call it miraculous. He was different than I had ever seen him before. . . .

I folded the letter quickly, as if to stop her voice, because it was Nancy I heard in my inner ear when I read her words. The feelings I had had that night in Washington were no less intense for the passage of time and the soporific Roman afternoon in which I read her letter.

But how could she know of Furey's offer, let alone that I had accepted it? The answer to that question was contained in Cassell's letter, dictated, typed, but unmistakably the product of his feverish mind. He knew I would understand it was the right thing to release to the press my acceptance of Furey's offer, which had been conveyed to him by Gilligan. This biography could be the way out of the woods for me as a writer. Cassell was reminded of the aborted nonfiction book, a post-conciliar survey, that had marked the beginning of our relations. I was smart to have set the thing aside then, but now I had a real hook on which to hang the presentation and assessment of the recent history of the Catholic Church.

There was more—the letter ran to two and a half single-spaced pages—much of it consisting of bad news: the rejection of the book we had spoken about in New York, what he characterized as a realistic look at my career, and the reiterated statement that the life of Connolly would lift me from the literary doldrums and set me off on a new and far more profitable track. Now was the time for me to hit the market with a nonfiction book, and he could think of no better way for me to change my luck than with this life of my old friend Connolly, whom Cassell to his regret had not had the pleasure of knowing.

Cassell's gloomy review of my career certainly seemed justified in the light of the rejection. I had never had a book rejected before, and I found the experience frightening. It was difficult not to take as gospel what Cassell had been trying to tell me, and my hope that I could simply switch to mystery novels and go on as before now seemed hopelessly naive. My whole literary career—to employ Cassell's lofty phrase—seemed the product of luck rather than talent. How had I managed to fool so many for so long? I was so depressed by his estimate of my situation that I could not work up a satisfying anger at his jumping the gun with his announcement of Furey's offer. Writing Connolly's life now seemed the one thing between me and financial disaster.

At the Abbadia Celestina I had had a fleeting thought or two on how Connolly's life might be told. The approach, it seemed obvious, had to be critical, but the tone was something else. Should the story be told with tongue in cheek or with moral indignation? Beyond such preliminary considerations I had not gone because it had never seriously entered my mind that I would write Connolly's biography. The setting in which I found myself that afternoon, with the churchy presence of Rome all about me, suggested an ironic juxtaposition of traditional doctrine and Connolly's lifelong effort to water it down or alter it.

I thought of St. Cecelia and her titular church just blocks away, with a white marble statue of the saint beneath the main altar. She lies on her side, turned away from the viewer, her hair swept up to reveal on her exposed neck the mark made by the executioner's sword in his first unsuccessful attempt to behead her. She was a martyr for the faith Connolly had sought to redefine. A contrast between Connolly and the Church's first martyrs was a possible structure for the biography. Across the centuries believers had held as true things Connolly rejected. Yet he had considered himself a champion of the faith. The only conclusion was that Connolly's faith was not that of the Christian tradition. Had he literally believed in eternal reward or retribution? No matter the nonsense of Nancy's claim, Connolly's soul existed now and, as Furey had remembered with relish, was getting the long postponed hearing on his views before the choir of the saints. That was the traditional belief, at least. But what had Connolly's been?

When I left the restaurant, I felt fated to write the life of my old friend. I had no real freedom in the matter. My juveniles had enjoyed their day in the commercial sun and been remaindered for a pittance. I could not count on a steady stream of royalty checks. Perhaps if I had saved while I was earning I would now be free, but that legendary rainy day had not seemed threatening when I was selling stories as fast as I could turn them out.

I unlocked the door of my apartment but could not open it because of the chain. The smell of pot drifted from within. I called Maria's name twice, loudly, but half a minute passed before she came to peer out and let me in.

"I'm back," she said, looking naughty. All the windows of the apartment and the doors to the balcony were open, but the smoke was unmistakably still there.

"So am I. Do you have any more of that?"

She pretended she did not understand. The bridge of her nose developed a single wrinkle when she frowned. I closed the door and replaced the chain.

"Pot," I explained.

"Do you want some?" I might have proposed some sexual innovation. She knew what I thought of drugs, hard and soft, and we had had the usual argument about alcohol and marijuana which ended badly when I told her she was hooked on both. Only once before had she smoked pot in my apartment. An absolute condition of her staying with me was that she give it up or at least indulge in it elsewhere.

She had a small cache of five joints which she produced almost excitedly, offering them to me as if they were an aphrodisiac. I took them from her, went into the bathroom and flushed them down the toilet. She had followed me and when she saw what I was doing, tried to stop me by grabbing my arm, but I pushed her out of the way, more energetically than I meant to. She fell back, lost her balance, grabbed the door and, when it swung shut, crushed her fingers.

"You sonofabitch. You rotten bastard." She held her injured hand in the other and stared at me with hatred, tears in her eyes. Then she flung herself at me, slapping my face, kicking at my ankles. When I grabbed her wrists, she brought her knee painfully up into my groin. I gasped and yelled something, I don't know what, and, still holding her wrists, backed her swiftly into the living room and flung her from me.

"I want you to take anything you have here and go."

"You're damned right I'm going. Just who do you think you are?"

"And I'll want your key."

My pain was beginning to subside. Maria's eyes dropped and she turned away. When she spoke again it was softly. "I'm sorry. My hand hurts."

"I hurt too."

She laughed tentatively. "It works, doesn't it? Basic antirape protection."

"I wasn't trying to rape you."

She came to me. "I'm sorry I kneed you."

"Maria, I spoke in anger, but I meant it. I don't want you to come here anymore."

"Are you afraid of Austin?"

Afraid. I was weary of her youth and, I suppose, of Austin's too. "Maria, I'm old enough to be your father."

"No, thanks. One is enough. I said I'm sorry and I mean it. I shouldn't have smoked here. I won't do it again."

"It's not just that."

"Where have you been?"

I had tried unsuccessfully to tell her I was worried about my writing, but I tried again. She seemed incapable of comprehending financial insecurity. She had some notion of how many books I had published and must have supposed that, if not rich like her father, I was nevertheless quite comfortable. It was my account of the Abbadia Celestina that caught her fancy. She hugged her knees and leaned toward me as I talked, and the mention of the reburied bones of the medieval monks made her shiver.

"Take me there."

"You haven't been listening. I am trying to start over again from scratch as a writer."

She sat on the floor next to my chair and looked up at me pleadingly. She seemed even younger than usual. "Wouldn't we be fun in a monastery together?"

"I live in the guest house." I was disappointed in her. Did she think that centuries ago men had lifted stone upon stone to provide us with an interesting place to make love? "Maria, I may give up this apartment."

"Why?"

"I can't afford it. The guest house at the abbey is free."

"Are you really broke?"

"Not yet. But unless I can write a successful book, I don't know what my future will be."

"But you write books all the time."

"For kids. I seem to have lost my appeal for youth." She began to stroke my ankle, bringing memories I did not want. "I've been asked to write a biography."

"Your life?"

"Not an autobiography. The life of my old friend Michael Connolly."

"He's an odd person, but I like him."

"That must have been a memorable lecture he gave at Loyola if you remember him so well."

"But he was here."

In the street below a car motor started up, voices rose, some in anger. I moved my foot but Maria's hand remained on my ankle.

"Michael Connolly is dead, Maria."

"Don't be silly. He was here yesterday."

"He died in a plane crash. We read about it one day at the Otello. It's why I went back to the States. Surely you remember that."

"Well, he said he was Michael Connolly and I was to tell you he was here." The topic lost interest for her. I found her caresses calculated. She did not want me to drop her; if nothing else she wanted to stay in this apartment.

"What did he look like?"

She thought about it. "Like you. Gray where you're blond. A little taller than you. I suppose it's the beard."

I relaxed. Michael Connolly had always been smooth-shaven. Of course, hair continues to grow after death. Someone must be impersonating Connolly. Had it been an old classmate, prompted to whimsy when my door was opened by Maria? I imagined him giving that name and hurrying away.

"Oh, he wanted to come in. Fortunately I had the chain on. He wanted to see you."

"What did you tell him?"

"The truth. I didn't know where you were."

"It must have been a practical joke, in very poor taste."

I wished I could explain away Nancy's story as easily. But who could have convinced her he was Michael Connolly? I found I wanted to drop the topic too. Phrases from Nancy's letter came to mind and with them the remembered sound of her voice. It was the conviction with which she spoke that was worrisome, indicating a reaction to Connolly's death more profound than I had noticed during the two days I stayed with her. She had been calm and relaxed then, at least on the surface. Had her resignation been a mask for despair that later gave rise to hallucinatory visitations? I was ashamed now that I had simply walked away from her. Her claim to have seen Michael was a plea for help and her letter echoed it.

The solace Maria's caresses promised was no longer unattractive. I put my hands on either side of her face and she got to her knees. I might have been giving her a blessing. I kissed her then and she came urgently and passionately into my arms.

Clouds rolled over the Alban hills and rain seemed not so much to fall as to become part of the landscape, heaven and earth inseparable. This thought had a mythic, reassuring effect as I directed my car up the mountain road, hunched over the wheel and peering through a windshield from which the wiper ineffectually swept the molten water. My decision not to spend the night in Rome with Maria was prompted by a phone call that came while Maria and I were still in bed. She reached for it and said Hello rather than *Pronto*. She listened for a moment.

"Austin, I am going to hang up this phone. Don't ever call here again, do you understand?"

Her mouth dropped open at his reply, and she hurled the phone from her. It lay at the foot of the bed, the boy's angry unintelligible babble dispelling the animal peace. The thought of picking up the phone and threatening to beat the hell out of him again was appealing, but in the end I reached for the receiver and hung it up. Austin had attacked me, Maria had too. I had not engaged in physical violence since childhood, so it was easy to blame these recent outbursts on them. Maybe that is the inevitable expression of middle-aged and youthful relations.

"Poor Austin," Maria said, the sheet pulled to her chin in odd postcoital modesty.

"Have you been sleeping with him?"

"That's a dumb question."

"Give me a dumb answer."

Her look was reproachful. "Do you want me to ask you about all the women you've slept with?"

"I am asking about one specific person."

"Even so."

Meaning yes, no doubt. If it meant little to Maria, it obviously meant much to Austin. On that, I sided with him. Casual sex is no solution to anything. Sex is not a solution. From a religious point of view, as I had been raised to believe, it is the problem. And so it is.

"I don't blame him for being jealous."

She made a face. "You still want to get rid of me."

"I want to rid you of me. There's a difference."

"Please. I don't want a lecture. Or a sermon." She sighed. "My mother always said men are ungrateful after you give them what they want."

"She's right."

She sat up, letting the sheet fall away from her breasts. Why should her body be given for my pointless pleasure rather than the begetting of children? Upbringing again. One does not shake the outlook of more than half a lifetime easily. It did not matter that Maria was my willing partner. Her life was worth more than I could give her, and if she thought she could indulge in years of hedonism and end up just where she had been before, she was wrong. No deed is unimportant. The thought seemed part of my rationale for writing Connolly's life. I would examine what he had been and done in the clear light of the Christianity he had tried to obscure.

"You don't believe that." She brought her body against mine, but satiety is a powerful defense.

"I'm going back to the abbey."

"Take me with you."

"I can't. I told you why. Life is a goddam lottery, Maria. I mean it when I say I'm in trouble as a writer. A year from now I could be a shoe salesman. I have to be alone and work. My life depends on it."

"I will not go back to Austin."

"Then stay here."

"You're going to give up this apartment."

"That can't be done immediately in any case."

"If you could, you'd throw me right out on my ass now, wouldn't you?"

Before the fulfillment of desire, her smutty tongue could stimulate me. Afterward, it only seemed pathetic.

"You knew it had to end sometime."

"Did I? I thought things were nice. I won't smoke pot again, Jim. Ever. That's a promise."

"That isn't the problem."

"Maybe I could raise the rent from my father."

"No." Did she want to turn me into a grizzled gigolo?

"How long will the apartment be yours?"

"Until you go back to the States."

"But I'm not going back."

Her embrace tightened. If she wanted to make love again she had the wrong man. Maybe the demented Austin was good for two in a row, but Austin was young. Maybe he was in love as well. I am sure he thought he was. As if in corroboration, the phone rang again. I answered it.

"Clark? I'm going to kill you."

"No, you're not."

"I'm saying it, and you'd better believe me. I'm going to kill you if it's the last thing I do."

"Maria and I have decided to call it quits. That's what we've been talking about."

Maria tried to take the phone but I turned my back to her. Austin said with a calmness I did not like, "That doesn't matter. You don't deserve to live."

"Who does?"

"Just remember what I say. Sometime, somewhere, I'm going to get you."

"Have you chosen your weapon?"

It was his turn to hang up. I put the phone down and told Maria Austin had decided to kill me.

"My God, Jim. He might try. He's not all there."

"He loves you."

"He's crazy." But she could not suppress her delight that one man had threatened to kill another over her. "Have I told you his story?"

Austin's story was very low on my list of things I wanted to hear, but I got it anyway, a story I flattered myself I could have written without benefit of the facts. Like Maria, Austin came from a broken home, but the break had occurred earlier. His father too had been the delinquent, and I had the uneasy feeling that I had been cast in his role to provide Austin an occasion for revenge.

"The poor kid."

"That doesn't give him a license to kill."

"True."

"Jim, you should get out of here. Go up to your abbey. He won't find you there."

I had wanted a way to escape from Maria, but this was not what I had in mind. Now it was I who said I would stay and Maria who urged me to go. I went, finally, but not before telling her, in a concession to her self-sacrificing air, the location of the Abbadia Celestina.

"Someday you'll take me there," she said, reading some script I did not have. But she needed some face-saving way to let me escape her, and I could grant her that. Our farewell, while tender, was chaste, and for the first time I really believed we were saying good-by.

I telephoned Nancy from the Hassler. Furey was not in, but asking for him gave me the right to attentions I did not deserve. The manager let me use the phone in his office, even got the overseas operator for me. And then, as if by magic, over thousands of miles and more than seven hours' flight time, I heard Nancy's voice.

"I got your letter."

"Jim, I think I should come over."

"What for?"

"We have to talk. Face to face. I want you to believe what I'm telling you."

"Nancy, I'm calling from the Hassler. I'm leaving Rome. Do you remember the Wilsons?"

"The Wilsons?"

"Ian and Milly. Once we went up to a country place they

have above Tivoli. An old medieval abbey, a renovated farmhouse."

"Is that where you'll be?"

"My writing is going badly."

"You mustn't write Michael's life."

I permitted some expensive time to go by. "Milly asked about you."

"Tell her I'll be seeing her soon."

"She and Ian are in England now."

"Are you writing that biography?"

"I think so."

"Michael will stop you if I can't."

"He dropped by my apartment in Rome."

"You've seen him!"

It was a dirty trick, but why should I further her madness by denying her claim? It seemed wiser to go along with her. But I did not want her coming to Rome. I suggested that Connolly might look her up again in Washington, and she should stay there just in case.

"Not if he's gone to Rome."

Couldn't Connolly show up anywhere he wanted in his present condition? The manager's office was a study in conspicuous consumption. The desk top was of black marble and the furniture reminded me of the stuff in VIP waiting rooms in Italian airports. Once in Milan I had won the right to wait out a long delay between planes in such a room by describing myself as an American poet. My unimpressive appearance sustained rather than questioned the pretense.

"Jim?"

"I am going up to the Wilsons' country place. Do you want the telephone number there?"

"Yes."

I gave it to her, feeling like a conspirator in a plot I had made up myself. The manager was insulted when I tried to pay him for the call. Doubtless he would put it on Furey's bill. And then I set off in the rain for Abbadia Celestina.

A life should be written truly, but what is truth? In the ensuing days I developed a grudging sympathy with Pontius Pilate. The life of Connolly that Furey wanted was, I suppose, as true as any other version, and it would have been easy to write it. Born of middle-class but honest parents, Michael Connolly, in the years immediately after his ordination to the priesthood, had conceived the ambition to make a name for himself, and how better than to cater to the subtle anti-Catholicism rampant in the media? Anti-Catholicism is the anti-Semitism of the liberal. By addressing himself to that in the guise of one concerned with true Catholicism, Connolly had a formula that could not fail. If only it had been that simple. I, alas, knew that, whatever his faults, Connolly had been sincere. This had been established in his first real encounter with Brady.

How to recall those days just before and in the early years of Vatican Council II? From our years in the seminary, Connolly and I had been made aware of a quickening of Catholic intellectual life, in England, in the United States—we were incorrigibly insular—and from that tutelage had sprung our devotion to Gilson, Maritain, Chesterton and others, notably Thomas Merton. But with John XXIII's call for *aggiornamento*, we had entered a completely new phase. Windows were to be opened, fresh air let in, new ideas welcomed rather than resisted. Connolly had written to me in Vietnam of things I scarcely understood.

Thomism, the thought of St. Thomas Aquinas, the hegemony of a thirteenth-century theologian, had, if Connolly was right, created the assumption that there was really nothing new under the intellectual sun, that all one need do when problems arose was seek their solution in the *Summa theologica*. According to Connolly, most of the textbooks used in the teaching of theology were written "according to the mind of St. Thomas," and that put the Church in a straitjacket. Evelyn Waugh published in *Life* an essay on the American epoch in the Catholic Church and stirred Connolly to opposition. The Italians, into whose hands, for accidental reasons, control of the Church had fallen, must be resisted. Connolly was making a name for himself as a young professor at Catholic University. The book he had fashioned from his doctoral dissertation at the Gregorianum had finally been published. And Brady hit the fan.

My only version of the story is Connolly's, but I have no reason to doubt it, and my anger was, if possible, greater than his. How dare the bishop attempt to suppress the first creative theological writing ever to appear in his diocese, if not in the United States?

"Orestes Brownson set the tone of American sycophancy," Connolly told me.

The occasion was another visit to Notre Dame, where Connolly was again teaching summer school. We had gone into the basement of Sacred Heart church and seen the grave of Brownson, the words on the stone worn almost illegible by the feet of the faithful. Brownson had been laid to rest in the middle aisle of the lower church.

"Brownson attacked Newman when the essay on development appeared. He had embraced God knows how many versions of Christianity and now he was the self-appointed defender of Catholic orthodoxy. Imagine, attacking Newman."

That day we had lunch with Father Hesburgh in the Morris Inn, seated at the president's reserved table in a corner of the raised section of the campus inn's restaurant. We had a nice view of the golf course and, throughout the meal, golfers hit errant drives within amused sight of the diners.

"Brownson received an appointment to the faculty here, but he died shortly after he arrived in South Bend," Hesburgh said. "He's buried in the church, you know."

Connolly told him we had visited the grave that morning.

"I say Mass within a few feet of it every day I'm on campus," Hesburgh said, as if conferring importance on the tomb. "It is one of my minor boasts that I have never, since my ordination, missed saying daily Mass. I've said Mass in hotel rooms in Moscow, at the South Pole, in Baja California, you name it." Hesburgh sipped his Manhattan.

"I wish I could say the same," Connolly said.

"It is a priest's major purpose in life."

"Jim is with *Alleluia*, Father."

"I have a subscription. I never miss an issue."

Theodore Hesburgh had been named president of Notre Dame in his early thirties and now, more than a decade later, he was still in place, not yet as renowned and popular as he was to become, but already someone to be reckoned with. Out of that lunch grew my profile of Hesburgh for *Alleluia*, as discussed a piece as I ever wrote. It was difficult, talking with the president of Notre Dame, not to share his serene conviction that his university was emblematic of the Church in America. He was remarkably unself-referential about this. He spoke of excellence as if it were an apple one could pick from an identifiable tree. And he was critical of the American Church.

"I studied in Rome myself," he told Connolly, and the remark was heavy with significance. "Do you realize what proportion of the population of the United States is Catholic?"

Yet where were the Catholic intellectuals and political leaders? Hesburgh acknowledged Gene McCarthy and Jack Kennedy, a good friend of his predecessor, John

Cavanaugh, but it was when he spoke of intellectual leadership that Hesburgh became truly eloquent. The piece I wrote concentrated on that. He was resolved to make Notre Dame a premier institution, and that would require an outlook different from the then reigning one. When he spoke of theological subjects, it was clear that Hesburgh and Connolly were on the same wavelength.

"Europeans, particularly the Italians, have no conception of ecumenism. They didn't grow up with Protestants and Jews the way we did."

I mentioned Waugh's article, but Hesburgh did not know it.

"I've written a book my bishop doesn't like," Connolly said.

I remember that Hesburgh encouraged him in somewhat delphic phrases. Sympathetic as the two priests were, there was something in Hesburgh that Connolly lacked, and that was unquestioning loyalty to the Church. I have never met a man with such confidence that everything is going to turn out all right. Perhaps that came from the never-missed daily Mass and the unembarrassed way he referred to the Lady under whose patronage his university was. There were those who saw a similarity between Hesburgh and James Shannon, the auxiliary bishop of St. Paul who later defected and married a divorcee, but that was a likeness that events disproved. Hesburgh remained a champion of clerical celibacy, and I for one never saw him in anything but clerical clothing. Connolly came away from that lunch with the conviction that he had received an imprimatur for his book more potent than any Bishop Brady could give.

"What does Brady intend to do?" I asked after we had said good-by to Hesburgh in front of the main building and gone down to a grotto that was a replica of Lourdes.

"Refuse me an imprimatur."

1 4 6

Those were still the days when Catholics and especially clerics were required to get a *nihil obstat* from someone appointed by a bishop whenever they wished to write on theological topics. Only then was an imprimatur granted. It was considered an act of defiance to publish any other way.

"What will you do?"

"Publish."

And he did, with Doubleday, despite the misgivings of Delaney, the religious editor. The book was more than successful, for a title with such limited appeal. It occasioned Connolly's first appearance in *Time*. He became a favorite of that news magazine, a Catholic to whom they could relate and whose prose, like theirs, was jazzy and effective. Brady summoned Connolly back from the Catholic University where he then was.

"I told him it was a matter of conscience, and that was what we talked about, conscience. Brady's idea of it is to do what you are told to do. He was furious when I cited examples of the saints defying ecclesiastical authorities. He asked me if I thought I was a saint."

"What was your answer?"

Connolly smiled. "No. A theologian. He said he was glad I recognized the difference."

It is safe to say that *The Ineffable God* established Connolly in the forefront of American Catholic theologians as well as among the mighties of the media. The main criticism of it was that it was historicist and recalled the worst excesses of modernism. No expression of the message Christ came to bring is sacrosanct, Connolly argued. Quite apart from the controversies as to when and by whom the Gospels were written, quite apart from the vagaries in the transmission of the texts, to say nothing of the difficulties attending translations into modern vernaculars, the good news cannot be identified with particular phrases, as if the believer's task were to quibble over words rather than to further the kingdom of heaven on earth.

It was an exciting book. Reading it with unconscious envy, I was impressed by what my old friend had done, and I applauded him in the pages of *Alleluia*. My voice was one of a chorus, and I take no credit for what *Time* termed his meteoric rise.

Brady delated Connolly to Rome, but in the halcyon days after the election of John XXIII Vatican bureaucracies no longer leapt at such opportunities. Connolly helped to bring about the revolution that put bishops in the dock of the theologians rather than the reverse. Nor was he unaware of what this revolution implied.

"They're chairmen of the board types, Jim. Give them a ledger and they have no peers. The great bishops of the United States were builders in a developing land. Parishes had to be established, and the economic credit of the Church put beyond the doubt of bankers. I don't take anything away from the John Carrolls, the Spaldings, the Hugheses and John Irelands. They were great men. But their time is long past. Not that you would know it from recent episcopal appointments. Look at McIntyre, for God's sake. Out of Wall Street into a cardinalate. If a bishop in this country has a higher degree, it's in canon law. How can these guys be the arbiters of theological argument?"

He spoke on the occasion of being summoned to Rome for an informal inquiry into his works, an invitation rather than a formal command, but one he was happy to accept. Paul VI was issuing caveats; he had already presented *Humanae Vitae* to the world, and the wide open Church of John XXIII seemed a thing of the past.

After a meal at L'Eau Vive, we went down to the offices of the National Catholic News Service in the Piazza della Pilotta, across from Connolly's old university, the

Gregorianum, where Connolly, the veteran now of many battles, was greeted as a hero. A young old man named Hanson, prematurely bald and looking as if he needed a shave once a week at least, was visibly impressed to have the famous Father Michael Connolly show up unannounced in his office.

"When did you get in? I had no idea you were in Rome."

"Haven't you read today's *L'Osservatore?*"

Hanson confessed that he had not.

"You'll find there an account of my first session with the inquisitors. The whole thing was supposed to be secret. I should have known better."

Connolly dictated then and there an amusing version of what had taken place in a high-ceilinged room on the Palazzo della Cancelleria the day before. If there is such a thing as impersonal vanity, he had it in an extreme form. Michael Connolly might be the ostensible object of the Holy Office's attention, but he was there as a symbol of much more, of the theology that had developed during and since the Council. Hanson had no difficulty accepting this interpretation.

Looking out over the Alban hills toward Rome, remembering that episode, it seemed to me that the revolution of the Catholic press was one with that of the theologians. We used to laugh about the old diocesan weeklies and the wire service that fed them from Washington. EARTHQUAKE IN MEXICO: NO CATHOLICS KILLED. BISHOP BRUMPUS TO VISIT OUR LADY OF THE SEVEN SORROWS. Such were the parochial headlines of yesteryear. The *National Catholic Reporter* led the way into a new era. Official Church documents came to be treated much as the *New York Times* treated the Pentagon Papers. The official was by definition suspect. The press was at once disengaged, judgmental and basically liberal. Bishops became figures of fun. The standard dichotomy of secular politics, conservative and liberal, became the procrustean bed on which was laid the news of the renewing Church. Any dissident nun or priest was presumed to be sincere, deserving of respect and sympathy. Every episcopal demur in the direction of traditional doctrine was severely criticized. John Deedy began his ineffable screeds on the inside cover of *Commonweal*. Anti-Catholicism became the note of the Catholic press. Michael Connolly's column was eventually carried in two hundred diocesan newspapers.

Lost in all this was the fact that the basic bone of contention was the resurrection of the dead. Even Connolly seemed surprised when I mentioned this.

"How do you understand that article of the Creed, Jim?" he asked me.

"My understanding of it isn't at issue."

"You're not smoking."

"I quit."

"Remember when the right to smoke conferred maturity on us? Was it in third year we were allowed to smoke?"

"Fourth. Are you still smoking?"

"Only metaphorically." He smiled. "That's rhetoric. I actually welcome this exchange."

We were in a bar on the Campo di Fiori, not far from the church of St. Bridget of Sweden. Connolly had undergone a third session with the commission of inquiry.

"Did Jesus rise from the dead, Mike?"

"Of course."

"If you believe that, why are you here?"

"Because that simple phrase can mean a number of things, and theologians have the right to explore its possible meanings."

"Such as?"

"What really happened in that upper room in Jerusalem? Did you ever see the place?"

"Have you?"

"Yes. It may or may not be the actual room. That is always a problem in the Holy Land. X marks the spot of the Annunciation, of the Ascension, of the Crucifixion. Even if the wrong spot is identified, the important thing is we're talking about an actual place. What precisely is the faith of the early Church? I mentioned the other night the amazing fact that the disciples who met Jesus on the road to Emmaus did not recognize him at first."

" 'Remember how our hearts burned within us when we walked with him on the way.' That's what they said afterward."

"Right. They had a very special experience. It was as though they had talked with the Lord and had a meal with him. They recognized him in the breaking of the bread."

"None of it literal?"

"I don't rule that out. The Apostles had the sense that, despite his death, Jesus was still with them. In spirit. The Paraclete. If a group of people said that today, how would we understand them?"

"If Jesus didn't literally rise from the dead, how about you and me?"

Connolly bought a package of Nazionale cigarettes. They came in a green package. "I smoked this brand as a seminarian. They're said to be made from street sweepings. That's not literally true."

That was the theme of the evening. The articles of the Creed meant something, but it was unlikely that it was their literal sense.

"Am I shaking your faith, Jim?"

"Nothing could."

"Good for you."

"I no longer have any faith to shake. I wonder if you do."

He smoked half a cigarette as if seeking a reply, but when he spoke he changed the subject to one less comfortable for me.

"How is Nancy?"

A flood of thoughts came when he asked that question. Were the vows he had witnessed when Nancy and I married open to his easy hermeneutics too, meaning anything but what we had literally said? The annulment Nancy had gotten suggested a casuistic approach to what we had pledged one morning in Manhattan in the presence of Michael Connolly and assorted friends. It all seemed of a piece, Connolly's creative theology and Nancy's bid to have our marriage declared null and void. Did Connolly interpret his promise of celibacy that way? I asked him if he had ever considered laicization.

"No. That's not a serious possibility for me. I can do more, in my modest way, right where I am. Nancy never got over the death of your son, did she?"

Nancy was a sore spot, but mention of Greg cut me to the bone. I considered my dead son a private matter.

I said, "She thinks of him as still existing, somewhere, somehow."

"He does."

"In our memories?" I thought of Nancy ridding the house of all reminders of our son.

"You make that sound unimportant."

The greatest temptation to my lack of faith was the desire to think of Greg as I had described Nancy thinking of him, an ethereal soul somewhere in outer space awaiting the *eschaton* when the dead would resume their bodies and live happily ever after. There was something compelling in that hope. How can we think of a dead person as we do a fallen leaf or even a loved pet? The dream of immortality is as old as the race. But if that meant only retention in the memories of the bereaved it was on a par with my images of Newman Hall.

"What will come of these meetings?" I asked him.

He shrugged. "God knows."

God. A supreme being without whose sustaining causality all else would revert to nothingness. God who had become flesh in Jesus of Nazareth. In Connolly's theology that and everything else in traditional belief was negotiable. It was a moment when I was happy I had lost my faith.

At the Abbadia Celestina my days assumed the routine they had had for years, but now in the morning after having had my tea I sat down to my typewriter not to invent an adventure story for boys but, on commission from Furey, to tell the story of Michael Connolly to a world that might very well not be interested in it.

Seated at the refectory table that had become my desk, looking out at hills amorphous in the morning mist, my mind seemed a slate on which nothing had been written, and so too did the sheet of paper in the carriage of my typewriter. My question was not, What is life? but, What is a life? Dates I had and episodes; I had at least the beginning of thematic development in the contrast between Connolly and the martyrs of the Church. Hanson had used the term "martyr" in writing his heated accounts of the inquisition in the Palazzo della Cancelleria. My prologue turned on that, inviting me to compare Connolly with St. Cecelia and Thomas More and others who had laid down their lives for the faith. There was little need to belabor the irony involved. Connolly had been in no danger of losing his life; his interrogators were not hostile pagans but custodians of orthodox Christianity. He was lionized in the press rather than fed to the lions. The Colosseum formed in my mind, and I compared its current ruined condition with the arena in which early Christians had been used to titillate the jaded appetites of Imperial Rome. The concept of martyrdom had deteriorated along with the Colosseum, that was my suggestion, and I warmed to my task.

Once begun, the book grew as other books of mine had grown before, five pages a day, a relentless production enabling me to calculate with exactitude when the draft would be completed. History is interpretation and so is biography. There is no neutral, uninterpreted recital of the facts. My viewpoint was that of the Catholic orthodoxy of my youth and of Connolly's too. This was a minor motif. The young Michael Connolly sitting in judgment on the theologian he had become. Call it progress or call it degeneration, the contrast was there, whatever my personal standpoint. Biography is also revenge, I suppose, but I resolved to be as fair as I could, keeping my unbelieving self out of the narrative, not letting the cuckold husband condemn the man who had seduced his wife.

Seduction is too sensuous a word for the intellectual excitement Connolly represented for Nancy. But flesh is not always the most direct way to a fleshly response. Did I dare a scene with Connolly and Nancy and myself at lunch in that hostaria on the Borgo Pio? Years of writing fiction had prepared me for the presentation of the truth. I took a page from Connolly's book. It was not the literal sense of what I wrote that conveyed the deep truth of the narrative.

One day I drove down to Tivoli for lunch, not wanting seclusion to become oppressive. Now that the book was under way I felt I deserved a treat. The restaurants of Tivoli were aswarm with tourists who had spent their morning marveling at the cascade of fountains in the Villa d'Este. But I found a small place far from the main square and enjoyed my meal in fitful sunlight. Clouds were gathering, rolling in from beyond the town. Long before I had finished eating the sky darkened, and at three o'clock the rain began. I had neither raincoat nor umbrella, and it became clear that this was not a storm that could be waited out. I made a break for the car and arrived at it dripping wet. The dry haven of the Wilsons' guest house was a compelling destination.

Outside Tivoli, the sky grew even darker, and the sound of the rain on the Fiat's roof was loud and angry. I was moving along at 20 kph and cursing myself for not staying put in the restaurant when headlights appeared, approaching at a great rate of speed. I gripped the wheel as my whole body tensed. The vehicle went by me with a roar that drowned out the rain, and a huge wave of water swept over the hood of my car. The little Fiat shuddered in the wake of the truck's passing, and I was so grateful to have avoided a head-on collision I was not even angry with the driver.

The road into the Wilsons', when at last I arrived at it, had begun to wash away under the torrential downpour, and I weighed the risk of sliding off it and rolling down the hill. On the left side of the road was the rise of the hill, but I could not hug it closely enough to prevent the right wheels from spinning in air where the road had washed away. Once near Assisi I had gone off a road like that, the car tipping crazily and then sliding with eerie ease into the ditch while Nancy screamed. The memory was sufficient to decide me to abandon the car and walk.

With the motor and windshield wipers off, the rain became a relentless roar. Condensation within and rain without made the windows impossible to see through. Listening to the racket, I imagined I could hear it slacken, but after ten minutes it was clear that the rain was coming down harder than before.

Rain swept into the car when I opened the door. Speed was the only solution. I jumped out onto the muddy road, pushed the door shut; but it did not catch, so I had to slam it again, hard, before starting to run toward the house. I had pulled up my collar without effect. Twenty yards from the car I was soaked through and through. The guest house became suddenly visible in a flash of lightning when I rounded the curve in the road. Running into an indistinct underwater world, I was propelled by the promise of warmth and shelter and a change of clothes.

The guest house door was open. My first thought was that it had blown open, but when I looked in at the shambles of the kitchen, I knew that someone had broken in while I was away. Halfway into the room, stepping over the stove which lay on its side, avoiding the food that had been dumped from the refrigerator, I stopped. Were they still here?

I cocked my head, but all I could hear was the storm. Anyone still in the guest house would not have heard me approach and enter. The rain created the same illusions that a shower does: I thought I heard voices though I was not sure. But I could not turn off the rain to find out. The refrigerator, its door open, inside light out, leaned against the table. I put my hand inside, but its temperature told me nothing of how long it had been unplugged. It seemed wiser to assume that the vandalism was recent.

I returned to the open door and stood just inside it, feeling the wind and rain on my back, reluctant to go out into it again, staring beyond the kitchen at the steps that led up to the middle room. There were muddy footprints on it. How long had it been since the rain began? I was now certain there were strangers in the guest house.

I turned and plunged into the rain and began to run back along the road to my car. I wanted only to get out of there. I would drive to Tivoli, telephone Ian and tell him his goddam neighbors were at it again. Because of the blinding rain, I did not at first trust my feeling that there was something odd about the car when I approached it. It seemed to list, but that could be because of the washed-out road. That was not the explanation. It was lower. The tires were flat, all of them. I was now so thoroughly wet that I no longer minded the pelting rain. I circled the car slowly to make certain that all the tires were flat. They were. And it was foolish to think that four tires would just go flat at the same time.

Standing in the rain, I did not feel the fear I had in the guest house, at least not the same kind of fear. The flat tires had the appearance of a practical joke, and I looked around as if my tormentors might be out there watching me. But no one could have seen any distance in this rain. I opened the door of the car and was about to get in when I stopped and examined the interior. It was empty. I got behind the wheel and pulled the door closed. I put the key in the ignition, fully intending to back out of there and ride the wheel rims to Tivoli, or at least to the first phone. But when I turned the key nothing happened. I tried it again. Nothing. There was only a metallic click, no reassuring sound of the motor starting.

It seemed clear that whoever had torn up the guest house had also let the air out of the car's tires and then done something to the ignition as well. Had the spark plugs been removed, or the distributor cap? The ways to prevent a motor from starting suddenly seemed infinite. The notion that this was a practical joke had never been a live possibility. Now it was an absurdity. I was furious with Ian for talking me into using his guest house when the place was apparently under siege from irate peasants. I thought of that boulder that had come rolling down the hill. Ian was mistaken if he thought he had settled his differences with the citizens of the town above the farm.

Sitting there in relatively dry security, I imagined the most likely sequence of events. Whoever had vandalized the house had heard the approach of the car and managed to get out of the guest house and under cover before deciding to make a run for it. When I went into the house, they had come out on the road, let the air out of my tires and done whatever they did to the ignition, then disappeared into the rain, secure in the knowledge that I could not pursue them. I unlocked the driver's door and pushed it open.

The rain was definitely less intense now. Not that it made any difference to me, soaked as I was. I started back toward the house. Walking. Why work up a sweat and increase my already present danger from pneumonia? The door of the guest house stood open as before. I went on past, down the steeply declining gravel road to the main house. Ian had given me a key, but I half expected to see the door of the main house standing open too. It was not. I let myself in, closed the door behind me and locked it.

Dear God, how dry and peaceful it was. The shambles of the guest house, the disabled car, diminished in importance now that I was in the reassuring familiarity of the house. I went upstairs to the second floor, intent on borrowing dry clothes from Ian's closet. I was rehearsing the phone call I would make to England after I got out of my soggy clothing. In the bathroom, I rubbed my hair and beard dry with a towel and found a robe hanging on a hook behind the door.

I left my clothes in a damp pile on the floor. After toweling my body, I slipped into the robe and immediately my spirits lifted. Now for a drink. But first I meant to telephone Ian. It would not do to sound too panicky and upset. Better to mimic Ian's own understated manner. The damage to the guest house would mean less when Ian learned that the main house had been spared.

At the top of the stairs was a large open area which was used as a television room. There was a liquor cabinet next

158

to the set. I opened it and poured two ounces of brandy into a glass. Having tossed that off in several swallows, welcoming the fiery descent of the liquid, I made myself comfortable on a large overstuffed couch, put the phone on the arm of the couch, lifted the receiver to my ear.

Outside there was the rumble of thunder. Involuntarily, I took the receiver from my ear. When I put it back again, I heard nothing, as if the line had been struck. I jiggled the cradle several times and even said "Hello" self-consciously into the silent instrument. The phone was not working.

The brandy helped, but taking more was inadvisable. What had to be avoided was irrational panic. Lightning had not struck the telephone wires. The statistical probability of that happening just when I picked up the phone was astronomically low. The wires must have been cut. If the phone in the guest house had been rendered useless, that would affect the whole system. Those who had tipped over a stove and refrigerator were unlikely to leave the phone intact. My hand lifted to the lamp beside the couch. With my fingers on the switch, I hesitated, closing my eyes. Addressing the Lares and Penates of the house, I prayed that the light would work. I turned the switch and opened my eyes. Nothing. Apparently there was no electrical power either.

The room was more dark than light. Even if the storm let up, there would be no more light that day. And no electric light. I saw that there was wood in the fireplace at the end of the room. There was the sound of rain in the chimney after I opened the flue. The fire had been carefully laid in preparation for the Wilsons' return. Night in the mountains was always cool and a fire was seldom unwelcome. I struck a match and lit the fire.

Within minutes my whole attitude had changed. The fire leapt and crackled and filled the room with its cheerful

159

glow. I poured another ounce of brandy and settled down in front of the fire. The damage done to the guest house and my car could be seen in perspective now. For Ian Wilson it would be an annoyance on a par with the bounding boulder. Seated in the main house, dry in a robe, the fire burning brightly in front of me, I thought of my manuscript in the guest house. What had happened to the life of Michael Connolly? Did I really care? That I might so easily dismiss the loss of days of intense work came as a surprise. What had been written once could be rewritten. Michael Connolly had become a product of my imagination, and I could summon him at will. The prologue, if destroyed, could be written better the next time. I had written only a rough draft, and the actual is always less than the possible. Brandy is a powerful agent of resignation.

I took the final drops from the glass on my tongue, trying to recall the crazy fear that had driven me from the guest house, out into the rain and back to my car. I was dealing with peasants, vindictive rustics; it was ridiculous to make what had happened more than it was. Had I locked the door when I came into the house? I could not remember. Doubt, once admitted, is inexpungeable. Before settling down for the night—I had no intention of returning to the guest house—I would have to make a tour of the house, checking doors and windows. Whoever had been undeterred by the storm could not be trusted to desist because of night.

Away from the fire, the sense of safety the brandy provided diminished. Going downstairs, descending into the dark, I kept to the side of the staircase, my hand on the railing. Rain continued to fall outside, but the wind had dropped, and against the background of a steady susurrus I strained to hear the sound of alien presences. But thieves by nature are silent, though the tearing up of the guest house must have been accompanied by an enormous racket.

I found the front door locked and groped my way through the downstairs, checking latches and locks. The locks on the French doors were so fragile as to be derisory, and several were unlocked. Now the absence of electricity seemed almost a blessing. If I had not been seen to enter the house, no one would know I was here. And then I remembered the fire.

I went through the house as quickly as I dared in the dark and mounted the stairs. He was standing before the fire.

"Hello, Jim."

I stood frozen in fear. He turned and his face was illumined by the jumping flames.

"Fear not, it is I."

I did not find the sound of Michael Connolly's laughter reassuring.

Connolly shivered and turned back to the fire, extending his hands toward it. He hunched his shoulders and seemed to tremble. As I had been, he was wringing wet. I joined him beside the fire.

"How did you find this place?"

"Nancy told me you'd be here if you weren't at your apartment."

This matter-of-fact explanation was a relief. "I went to your funeral."

He said nothing.

"The burial at Newman Hall was very nice. You would have liked it."

He made a noise, a grunt, a laugh, a moan.

"This wasn't an easy place to find," he said.

"When did you get here?"

"When? I just got here. I took a cab from Tivoli."

"In this storm?"

"The driver wanted to turn back but I convinced him not to. The storm was behind us as well."

"I'm surprised he found the place."

"So was he."

Thus blandly did I converse with a man supposedly dead. The shock I had felt when I first saw him silhouetted in front of the fire and the fear when he turned and I saw who he was subsided.

"Would you like a drink?"

"What do you have?" He leaned toward the fire and began to rub his hair and beard.

"I'm having brandy."

"Sounds good."

He took his glass in both hands and shivered again. I might have suggested he put on some of Ian's dry clothes, but at the moment it was not the comfort of Michael Connolly that seemed important.

I said, "Tell me about it. What happened?"

Part Three

Chapter 1

This is the way that Michael Connolly died.

He had checked in for the Washington flight at the gate, received his seat assignment, and gone into the waiting area carrying the single bag he restricted himself to so as not to have to dally at the baggage claim when he arrived at his destination. Sun was bright at the large plate-glass windows, and when he put down his bag he had to shade his eyes against it. He opened the copy of the *Chicago Tribune* he had bought, then closed it again. He did not want to read. The lecture he had given, the discussion period, the relentless hospitality of his hosts, had left him weary. He sat among the salesmen and tourists and assorted travelers and tried not to think of the work awaiting him at home.

"Lectures, Jim," he said to me. "My God, the lectures I've given. If they were all laid end to end you couldn't make head nor tail of them. And I had a deadline for a new book. I tried to write the lectures so they would be usable in the book, but even so I felt overextended."

The boredom of waiting for the flight to be called, the heat of the sun, the excited chatter around him, made him check his watch. Did he have time to dash for a drink in the twenty minutes left him? He decided to try it, leaving his bag in the waiting area, taking only a thin brief case. There were long lines at the check-in counter. He asked no one to look after his things.

Hurrying toward the main terminal and the stand-up bar, he was going against the grain of a ceaseless flow of people heading for their boarding gates. The stand-up bar halfway to the main terminal was mobbed. He looked with despair at the throngs pressing into the little alcove where two bartenders tried to fill the shouted orders, splashing imperfectly proportioned drinks into plastic cups already filled to the brim with ice. The indignity of taking a supposedly leisurely drink in such circumstances repelled him. He decided to continue to the main terminal and the cocktail lounge. No fellow passenger would want the physical burden of a stolen bag, never mind the moral burden.

He took the escalator to the cocktail lounge, asked a harried waitress to bring him a Bloody Mary and settled into a chair. A quick drink in comfortable surroundings, no elbowing others like a pig at the trough. He refrained from looking at his watch. It would be close but he would not miss his plane. The waitress did not fail him. His drink arrived before a minute had passed. What he did not count on was the woman who tumbled to the floor with a strangled cry, her skirt riding up and exposing fat upper legs. Her purse spilled its contents on the carpet and the pale blue beads of a crystal rosary glistened in the sunlight laid in bars across the lounge by the window blinds. Connolly put down his drink and joined those who had risen to surround the fallen woman.

His priestly life had not involved much pastoral work, sick calls had formed no regular part of his duties, but the twisted face, the jerking movements of the woman's head, her lolling tongue, made it clear that this was something more serious than a fainting spell. Connolly knelt beside her.

"Do you want a priest?"

Her eyes opened, rolled, focused on him. The question seemed to calm her. The sound that emerged from her lips seemed interpretable as assent.

"Are you sorry for your sins?"

Her eyes dropped to his necktie and rose to search his face. Her mouth began to work and then she said, "A priest."

"She wants a priest," someone behind Connolly said.

"The chaplain. Call the chaplain."

"I am a priest," Connolly said to the fallen woman.

She shook her head and turned away from him. The strange jerking motions resumed.

"Are you sorry for your sins?" Connolly repeated.

A hand was laid on his shoulder. "Are you a doctor?"

Connolly looked up at a frowning face. "I'm a priest."

Suddenly he was aware of the disbelief and anger in the faces of those looking down at him. A waitress announced that the airport chaplain was on his way. The man who had asked Connolly if he was a doctor, a portly man in a three-piece suit with a pre–Vatican II look about him, attempted to pull Connolly to his feet. "She said a *priest*."

Connolly turned back to the woman. Whatever was happening to her had worsened. He should give her absolu-

1 6 7

tion. Incredibly he could not remember the words. His mind was a room bare of furniture, swept clean by the hostility and anger of those ringing him and the woman. Hands were laid on him and he was pulled back. He sat on his heels, but the pressure continued and he would have fallen if he had not got hold of a chair leg and stopped himself. The indignant man stepped between Connolly and the woman. Connolly got to his hands and knees, more alarmed by his inability to recall the words of absolution than by the small violence that had been done him. He struggled to his feet just as the little group made way for the arrival of the chaplain. The man had a small head with graying hair and, although he wore a cardigan sweater, the Roman collar made him unequivocally a priest. Connolly moved away as the chaplain swiftly prayed over the woman and lifted his hand in blessing.

He returned to his table and the drink he no longer wanted. The episode had made him feel unfrocked, fraudulent, impotent. He held his drink, watching the little chaplain perform his function with authority, commanding embarrassed respect from the onlookers. It was fully five minutes after the chaplain appeared that the medical team arrived. More authoritative activity. Connolly heard epilepsy mentioned, and concern was expressed about the woman's tongue.

"She might swallow it."

"Everybody step back, please," one of the medics said. But it was the chaplain who dispersed the crowd. The man in the three-piece suit turned, saw Connolly, and glared malevolently at him. He approached his chair.

"What the hell were you trying to do?"

The man's back was to the huge bright window that looked out at the field. Connolly did not answer him. After a moment, the man made a disgusted sound and left. The woman was borne away on a stretcher, the chaplain following, and within a minute the large sunny room was only a cocktail lounge again.

Connolly sat there, trying but unable to dismiss what had happened. He had felt like an impostor even before he was treated as one. I am a priest, he had told the epileptic woman. Had it been the tone of his voice rather than what he wore that explained her skepticism? It was absurd to think that a Roman collar makes one a priest. Anyone can put on a collar. When he had stopped wearing them it was because so few priests on campuses did anymore, except on very special occasions. It had been the path of least resistance to dress like the rest of men; he had been conscious of no ideological motive for discarding clerical clothes. If he had a theory, it was that dress did not matter. But clearly it mattered when an emergency arose in a public place. Anyone could wear a Roman collar, anyone could claim to be a priest. But he had not remembered the formula of absolution.

How long had it been since he heard confessions? How long had it been since he himself confessed? The once weekly practice had dwindled to an infrequent event. Private confession, the whispering through a grille in a dark booth, had been a target of reformers, and he had followed the debate and apparently been more influenced by it than he realized.

When he remembered his plane, he rose in a panic. Throwing money on the little table beside his undrunk Bloody Mary, he left the lounge, ran around the circular upper balcony to the stairway, and hurried down it. He had to go through the security check again and inevitably there were lines. He might have attempted to go ahead of the others, crying out that he was late for his plane, but the fear that he might be doubted again stopped him. He inched forward and finally stepped through the bogus little doorway of the security check. It was all he could do not to break into a run as he headed down the long passageway to his gate. His pace slowed rather than quickened. He was certain his plane had left.

And so it had. The waiting room was empty. The airline attendants had left the counter. His bag was where he had left it. He picked it up and walked indecisively back toward the main terminal. His destination seemed to be the ticket counter. His ticket had been taken when he checked in for the flight and received his seat assignment. Surely they would replace it when he explained that he had missed the flight. He could leave on a later one. But when he came into the main terminal and saw the sign indicating that an interdenominational chapel was located in the basement, he thought of the small gray-haired priest in the cardigan. His brother in the cloth—except that Connolly did not wear the cloth. He pressed the button for the elevator.

When he emerged into the subbasement, an arrowed sign told him where to go. The chapel was reached by going down what seemed a heating tunnel, exposed pipes overhead, an odd echoing overheated corridor down which Michael Connolly carried his bag. The doors of the chapel were open. Uneven rows of chairs surrounded the altar on three sides. At the back of the chapel was an opening where several workmen and a waitress were having coffee and doughnuts. The waitress looked at Connolly without interest.

Connolly took a chair. Opposite the altar a banner on the wall said Community of Our Lady of Loreto. Loreto? Shouldn't there be two t's? The House of Loretto, translated miraculously from the Holy Land to that town in Italy, said to be the home of Jesus, Mary and Joseph. The ceiling of the chapel was false, imperfectly concealing more pipes. His mind was as blank as it had been when he tried to give the woman absolution. He did not know how long

1 7 0

he sat there. When the waitress left, she stopped to tell him that Mass had already been said, at 11:30. He nodded as if she spoke a language he did not know. It was the return of the chaplain that snapped him out of it.

The priest nodded at Connolly, looking disponible, but went on to the back room where two of the coffee drinkers still sat. Connolly could hear their voices, imperfectly audible, the words indistinct in this eerie underground atmosphere. He left. When the elevator deposited him on the main floor of the terminal, he had made up his mind that he would not try to get on the next flight. There was a hotel at the airport. He would take a room and deal with the airline by telephone.

The hotel was the airport Hilton and he reached it by taking a down escalator, a moving belt and then an up escalator to the registration desk. More lines, but he was no longer in a hurry. Registered, given a key, he took the elevator to his floor and walked down a long curved, carpeted corridor past doors with oversized numbers on them. He hung the Do Not Disturb sign on the outside knob before locking and bolting his door.

It was a corner room, all the drapes pulled. He lay down on the bed, wanting a moment's rest, but now he realized how tired he was, and when sleep came he welcomed it.

To die, to sleep, and by a sleep to say we end the heartache . . . The quotation that began in his head when he closed his eyes would not finish itself, and he pursued it through the scrambled restless dreams that followed as if it were the forgotten formula of absolution.

When he awoke in the darkened room, it was a full minute before he knew where he was. The sound of planes taking off provided the needed clue. He turned on the light beside the bed but did not get up. How easily he could fall asleep again. Why not? He felt that he had been freed from his schedule with impunity. He liked the thought that he had escaped, if only temporarily. When he closed his eyes, sleep did not return. He put out the light but that did not help. Finally he swung his legs off the bed, turned on the light again and sat listening to the ceaseless sound of takeoffs and landings. Yawning, he got to his feet and switched on the television.

To the news.

And that is when he learned that he had died in a plane crash in Washington.

While Connolly was telling me this story in the Wilsons' country house the storm abated, the electricity came on, and the lamps I had tried to light at either end of the couch cast their glow in competition with the fire on the grate. The atmosphere of the upper room and the flickering fire, his meditative tone, one of awed amusement, increased my sense that I was hearing a tale like those told when all history was oral and the words were to be remembered and passed on, gathering significance with the succession of generations. There was little doubt that Connolly regarded his improbable escape from death in that plane crash as something of deeper significance than luck, and I was ready to pounce on any suggestion that the whimsical hand of God had been at work that day at O'Hare, but none came.

I was sitting on the couch and Connolly, having first wrapped himself in the blanket thrown over it, settled in a chair beside the fire. He did not look at me as he talked. I might have been eavesdropping.

"When did you grow the beard?" I asked. It seemed best to keep to the inconsequential.

He put his hand to his face. "I just stopped shaving."

"That's a pretty good way to grow a beard."

"It turned out to be useful after I found your passport at Nancy's."

"And my credit cards?"

"It seemed unwise to travel under my own name."

"Why?"

A log snapped in the fireplace. Outside, water dripped from the eaves. "I don't know."

"How did you get to Washington?" I could not say, "To Nancy?"

"By bus."

I thought of reading of the plane crash in the Otello while having lunch with Maria; I thought of the ceremony at the National Shrine and the burial in Wisconsin. "It took you long enough."

"Oh, I didn't leave immediately." He pulled the blanket more tightly about him. "I stayed for nearly a week at the O'Hare Hilton before I started east."

"You liked being dead?"

"It has its attractions."

He fell asleep in the chair eventually and I left him there, taking a bed in a guest room for myself. The house no longer held any terrors for me with the resurrected Connolly asleep by the dying fire, but I left a lamp burning in the bedroom when I turned in. The room was at the back of the house. Its double windows looked out at the spectral ruins of the medieval abbey. The walls of the room were chalk white and, lying on my back, I stared at the raftered ceiling. What the hell was Connolly up to?

I had voiced no reaction to his story, neither surprise nor happiness, not anger either, though I had felt something of all three. It was anger that persisted. He had been altered by what had happened to him, as why shouldn't he be, but concealing the fact that he had survived was not among the things that had just happened to him. That was a matter of decision. Why had he preferred a phony death to letting the world know he had not been on that plane?

The reasons that occurred to me were not conducive to sleep. Some distance away, in the guest house, were the no-doubt scattered pages on which I had begun to write the life of Michael Connolly. Would he have heard of the project? I could imagine that it was the commissioned biography that had brought him through a storm into these hills to talk to me, but he had made no mention of it as he talked beside the fire. If he intended to go on playing dead, why should he assume he could entrust his secret to me? It had been a bad moment when he mentioned Nancy, but I had remained silent. Habit is powerful and I had never confronted him or Nancy with my knowledge of their betrayal of me. Lying sleepless in the guest room, I felt half an accomplice in their affair, my silence about it on a par with Connolly's concealment of his survival. I was still awake when the sound of bells drifted across the valley and nearby a cock crowed and then another. I waited but there was not a third.

The shambles of the guest house had to be dealt with before breakfast was welcome. Connolly helped me to restore order and showed no curiosity about what had happened. After we got the refectory table upright and replaced it by the window, he said, "Did you hear the bells?"

"They're my alarm clock."

"How long have you been up here?"

"Didn't Nancy tell you?"

"No."

I began to pick up my typewritten pages from the floor. Rain had come in the open window and they were sodden but salvageable. Thank God the intruders had not decided to tear them to pieces.

"Is there any wine?"

"Isn't it a little early for that?"

"This table would make a good altar. I'd like to say Mass."

"There's wine in the kitchen."

I left him alone. I went outside to where the morning sun promised to absorb the moisture left by the storm and walked out to the abbey. Connolly saying Mass at the table on which I had been writing his life was an odd thought. I had taken the typewritten pages with me lest he read them and learn what I was working on. The project made little sense now that Connolly was still among the living. That was what Nancy had meant. Suddenly I seemed to have a vested interest in Connolly's deception. At least until I finished my book. Furey's hope for an exposé now had a more solid foundation. A man who faked his own death would be far easier to handle than a dissident theologian bent on repudiating what he professed to believe. Connolly's writings were beyond the ken and interest of most readers, but what he had done since learning in that room in the O'Hare Hilton that he was thought dead was something more dramatic and understandable.

At Newman Hall we had both read a little book called *Brother Petroc's Return*, a minor Catholic novel that told of a resurrected medieval monk. Did Connolly envisage a noisy reentry after several months of presumed death? Would he dare allow it to seem a miracle? Standing in the ruins of the Abbadia Celestina, I looked back at the guest house where Connolly was saying Mass and felt this suspicion slip away. Last night, talking by the fire, he had not sounded like a charlatan, and this morning, helping me to clean up the guest house, he had been subdued and tranquil. I was reminded of Nancy's manner when she told me Michael had come to see her. I would have preferred to think Connolly planned a splashy news conference at which he would return to the media wonderland and attract global attention. What if he intended to remain dead?

I stayed away long enough for him to finish his Mass. When I returned to the guest house he was in the kitchen putting water on the stove. He might have been myself, assuming my routine, become himself the Wilsons' guest. The beard increased the illusion and I remembered Maria saying he resembled me. Perhaps he did. Apparently he had no difficulty using my passport. Gray hair looks blond and a beard is a kind of mask, of course, conferring anonymity as well as a kind of similarity.

"Make yourself at home," I said.

"What a great place this is. I don't wonder that you prefer it to your apartment."

"I work well here."

"What are you writing?"

"A mystery."

"I've been doing a bit of writing myself."

"Finishing your book?"

"No. Not a book. A notebook. I bought a spiral notebook in the terminal and filled most of it before I left O'Hare."

"Retreat notes?"

He smiled. "Remember those?"

During the annual retreat at Newman Hall and the major seminary, we had been advised to keep notes of the conferences and our own reflections. If there is a more unnatural kind of writing than that, I do not know of it. Of course we were supposed to be developing a spiritual life, that was part of preparation for the priesthood, but to sit down and write about one's soul seemed presumptuous, as if one were a Teresa of Avila or Thomas a Kempis. Come upon weeks or months later, those feverish pages were an embarrassment to read. In the unreal atmosphere of a retreat, the world recedes from view, and it is possible to imagine a future wholly unlike the past. The intensity of a retreat cannot last, perhaps it is not meant to, but it was the meagerness of its residue in later months that made it seem, in retrospect, mere pretense. I remember one retreat during which distraction at prayer seemed my besetting sin. I pondered long and unctuously how I could put myself more thoroughly in the presence of God when I prayed. Distraction at prayer. Good God. Had there really been a time when that was the worst I could accuse myself of?

Connolly's reaction to the abbey when I showed him around increased my sense that he would like to take my place there, as if assuming my identity had become a habit with him. He said little, but it was obvious he was affected by the place. For ten minutes he stood staring at the faded fresco on the refectory wall that no longer supported a ceiling. But, as was to be expected, it was the plastic bags of bones in the crypt that fascinated him most. I held up the plywood cover and he looked down until his eyes became accustomed to the darkness and he could make them out.

"They were collected from all around the ruins and reburied there."

"Reburied by whom?"

"The priest in the village up there."

He looked up to where the top of the steeple was visible over the lip of the hill, but his eyes went back to the bones in the crypt. What he then did should not have surprised me, but it did. He lifted his hand and traced a blessing over the reburied bones. I dropped the plywood sheet and it made a strange sound, like a distant detonation, and dust puffed from its edges.

"I hope they didn't mistake that for the Last Trump," I said.

"Do they play cards in purgatory?"

Once I would have taken that as skepticism about the halfway house between earth and heaven, but there was no irony in his voice. My remark had been half-hearted anyway. Why should I be bothered by the spectacle of a priest getting religion? But Connolly was not just another priest. He was a man who had made a career out of dissent and casting doubt on basic Christian beliefs. Beliefs about the resurrection for one, and here he was blessing those plastic bags of bones as if he believed that, in the future, the men who had lived and died in the abbey centuries ago would be called forth from the grave. That meant that those bones down there would live again.

"When do you plan to rise from the dead?" I asked as we went back across the lawn.

"Is that a swimming pool?"

"There are tennis courts too."

He squinted at me. "You should be in better shape than you are, living here."

"Want to play a set?"

We played tennis barefoot on the clay court. The bare feet were meant to take away the advantage I supposedly had wearing Ian's tennis shoes when Connolly had none. It had been years since I played tennis, and I had never been much good. Connolly on the other hand was an athlete, and I suppose such skills never completely desert one. Losing would not have been so bad if I had not wanted to beat him so badly. Are games always symbols of some other struggle? My only consolation was that he seemed to be more exhausted than I was when we decided to call it quits.

"I wish there was water in that pool," he said.

"There's a good shower in the main house."

"I may take a nap afterward."

A nap in midmorning? Well, why not? The dead have no duties. With Connolly out of the way I could get to work.

But work was the life of Connolly. What else did I have? Sooner or later, he would have to let people know he was alive, and it was possible that would cause a sensation, at least for a while. A man returned from the dead should be good for several days' attention by the media before the subject lost interest. A book appearing at the right time could profit from the noise. It gave me little pleasure to think that my career as a writer was now dependent on Connolly's life. Of course I could take another try at a mystery, but I did not want to forfeit Furey's twenty thousand. Like it or not, I was Connolly's biographer, my task more complicated now that he was alive. I remembered the notebook he had filled in Chicago.

It was at the bottom of the bag he had brought over from the main house that morning. Spiral binding, red plastic cover, lined pages. There was a Carson, Pirie, Scott sticker inside the back cover. $1.79. I sat at the refectory table and opened the notebook.

Hotels are the cemeteries of the half-dead. We used to joke about burying people in layers in the same grave, to save space. Instead there are now vertical marble file cases in which the deceased are shelved. The O'Hare Hilton is like that. To get here from the terminal I didn't have to go outside but down two flights by escalator where I could be conveyed by moving belt to the underground floor of the hotel. Travelers are for the most part content with the speed of the belt. To walk on it gives a bodiless sensation. With shoulder bags and suitcases and odd bits of luggage, silently and swift, travelers are moved beneath the earth to the hotel. I had not thought death had undone so many. Charon's boat become a moving walkway. The Registration Desk is busy even in the wee hours. Those checking in are largely salesmen. "I have a reservation," the man ahead of me announced importantly, as if he were included in the Book of Life.

8002 is neither the eight thousandth and second room nor does it seem to be on the eighth floor. A corner room. Two whole walls of window, nothing but window, all covered with drapes. My first thought was that people in glass houses shouldn't throw stones. The memory is chock full of banalities. Beggars can't be choosers. Finders keepers, losers weepers. But it was the one about glass houses that came to me, like a text for a homily. I opened the drapes and looked out at the vast expanse of the airport. A great many land vehicles seemed to be moving around out there. I look out at the field now. 6:45 AM. United—TWA—Flying Tigers—Northwest Orient. That sounds like boxing the compass. A Mexicana Airways plane. The elongated terminal building is all gray and white and out on the field a red and white checkerboard structure. Ralston Purina. People in glass houses. I pull the drapes shut and realize I am going into retreat.

I live in a glass house and I have made a name for myself by throwing stones. The sound of jets is unending. This room, this room, 8002 in a building containing God knows how many sleepers, dead to the world, the modern world. O'Hare and 8002 are the modern world. The furniture, simple as children's drawings, stick figures, is silver. So is the wall at the head of the double bed. The bed has three pillows. Don't think about that. The television gives a blurred rolling picture. Royal blue pile carpet and lamps of stainless steel with milk white plastic shades. The bedspread and drapes are yellow and white, a trace of green, the motif picked up in the uniforms worn by the maids. Is this the modern world in which the Church is to take her place?

The Church is already here. In the terminal, several levels underground, there is a chapel where Mass is said. Two things happened there. The text of the Mass I attended after hearing the news of the crash. "It is not that we have loved God but God has first loved us." And the responsorial psalm, read by an airport baggage clerk without apparent understanding, like a school kid called on to recite, one word after the other, as if each were a sentence in itself. Watching him, listening, I did not ask myself how profound his participation in the liturgy was. My own shallowness overwhelmed me when he read,

"Blessed is the man whose sins are forgiven." Down there beneath the concrete and roar of O'Hare I imagined the chapel was a catacomb, something buried and hidden away. That is how the Church is present, simple people, ticket counter clerks, maintenance men, a girl from a rental car agency, waitresses, some travelers passing through. *Aggiornamento?* What windows could be opened on the world if the Church is underground? I felt like a spy, a double agent at best. Was I one of them or one of the indifferent thousands up above on ground level?

The missals in the chapel are the leaflet kind. The first time I went down there I sat as far back from the altar as I could get. Rows of folding chairs arranged in a U around the altar. I wanted to be unobtrusive. What would these people think if they knew who I was? I actually imagined them being impressed. Michael Connolly, famous theologian. They would not have recognized my name, not those people. Who am I to presume to be their spokesman? They want a quick Mass, a moment of half-distracted prayer, and then back to work. Maybe the travelers are bargaining for a safe flight. Fulfilling an obligation, half superstitious, truly devout, there are a million points on the spectrum, but we are sinners all. Blessed is the man whose sins are forgiven. Have I thought much of the fact that I have sins to be forgiven? I was overwhelmed by the thought that I had become famous doing something trivial. Trivial and destructive. Did anything I have written or said speak to those people gathered in a catacomb under O'Hare airport?

After I heard about the crash on TV and later when I saw my name on the list of the dead, I wanted to announce to the world that Michael Connolly was still alive. I would call the Chicago newspapers. What publicity there would be. Shallow, shallow. I had punched three digits on the phone before I hung it up again. A jet lifts into the gray morning sky, its wing lights winking, dragging its noise up into the clouds. Among the dead Father Michael Connolly, dissident theologian. Of all the photographs they might have used, they came up with the stilted studio portrait I had taken for the jacket of *The Ineffable God*. Mine was one of dozens of square-inch photographs the *Sun-Times* ran. It might have been a page from a school yearbook. I felt dead and gone. I walked the whole length of the terminal conspicuously holding that paper as if someone must surely recognize me. Like a ghost, I was invisible. And I enjoyed it. Say that, write it down, think about it. I was excited to be part of a macabre joke, and the thought of prolonging it first came to me as a sort of stunt. Don't dispel the illusion. What fun to be dead for a while and then rise to notoriety. I went back to the O'Hare Hilton and 8002.

I am sure it is extraordinary for anyone to spend more than eight hours in the O'Hare Hilton. Everyone is between planes. Yet no one shows the least curiosity about my staying so long. Well, maybe the least. The maids seemed puzzled in an uninterested way. Guests must all look alike to them anyway.

My stay here has become a retreat in the old sense. I no longer ask myself what the Church should do in the modern world or how we must learn the lessons of modernity. 8002 is appropriately uncomfortable for long tenure. As often as not I sit up in bed and think and write in this notebook. I do not think of liberal and conservative positions on this or that. The underground chapel makes such contrasts puerile. Why do people go down there? To receive the body and blood of Christ. Why? Because he died for our sins. And rose again from the dead on the third day. My writings are a mockery of their faith. I think of the confidence with which I jousted with Parezzi and Morello in the Palazzo della Cancelleria. They were bureaucrats disturbed by the dilution of their product, no doubt about that. But I can't ignore the fact that my books were not written for anyone who prays in the O'Hare chapel. As we talked, Parezzi, Morello and I, though I did most of the talking, I felt I was twisting the noses of professors at an oral exam. Brady's perhaps. I was looking forward to giving my version to journalists. What if I had really died in that plane crash?

In the coffee shop here the social layers are clear. Irish waitresses, Spanish-speaking busboys, Oriental and black cooks. But there is a black at the cash register and a lithe lovely Japanese hostess in green jacket and beige slacks and what look to be patent-leather high heels. A washed-out redhead exchanges Polish jokes with a Mexican busboy. Suited chubby salesmen sit at the counter looking tired beneath their sprayed hair-dos. Their hair reminds me of members of the campus ministry who strike poses against the commerce their look-alikes engage in. The amount of food thrown away! I am surprised the place is not picketed by appalled clerics.

A sound in the kitchen made me turn guiltily, the note-book still in my hands. Connolly stood in a spot of sun-light, stretching and yawning.

"I could sleep forever in this mountain air, Jim."

And then he saw the notebook in my hand. A slight lift-ing of his eyebrows was the only change in his expression.

"No secrets here in the mountains," I said.

"Have you read any of it?"

"Some."

He came up the step into the middle room. His corduroy jacket and suntans had been in bad shape from being soaked in the rain but sleeping in them had made them worse. "I suppose the dead have no rights. May I?"

He shook a cigarette from the package lying on the refectory table and lit it deliberately.

"You can't have secrets from your biographer."

A nimbus of exhaled smoke enveloped him and for a moment he reminded me of the fading Christ on the refectory wall.

"How many volumes do you plan, Jim?"

"I'm serious."

He laughed, but there was a question in it. I lit a cigarette of my own and told him of Furey's offer. He seemed more amused than angry. In justification, I told him of the nosedive my writing career had taken.

"How much money can you make from a biography?"

"You'd be surprised."

"But Furey?" He looked thoughtful. "Have you begun it?"

I pointed to the pile of pages on the table. He drew it toward him, glanced at the top page, turned to the next, then leafed through half a dozen. He looked at me.

"A hatchet job?"

"Does it sound like one?"

"Maybe. I've never had a biography written of me before. No, that's not true. But the first one was most uncritical. Were you going to end it with my death?"

"That was the idea. Your miraculous escape provides a better ending."

He frowned. "I told you what happened. Read the notebook. The whole thing was a fluke."

"It's your keeping quiet about it that adds drama."

"What should I do, Jim?"

"Oh, there are lots of possibilities. You could hide out until next Easter and then make an appearance in St. Peter's Square."

"I'd be lost in the crowd. I've been lost in the crowd for a month. I've come to like it."

"The notebook reads like a general confession."

"Does it?"

"The portions I've read. Your deep thoughts in the chapel at O'Hare."

"You used to scold me about my writings. Why?"

"You know why."

He put out his cigarette. "That's why I came here to talk with you. You were always someone I could talk to."

"Newman Hall? It was quite a shock going back there. All those bright-eyed fundamentalists."

"Did you get to the part where I mention Aquinas?"

"Tell me about it."

"Toward the end of his life Thomas stopped writing, saying that everything he had written was straw. I changed that to crap in my own case." He took another cigarette from my package and looked at it. "I haven't smoked for months."

"They may be dangerous to your health."

He lit the cigarette. "There are advantages in being posthumous."

"Are you suggesting that you want to recant?"

"To whom? Should I go over to Castel Gandolfo and tell the pope I'm sorry?"

"Are you?"

"I've had a lot of time to think since I died. Not all of it is in that notebook. I would do a lot of things differently."

"Well, now you've risen from the dead."

"A parody of my own theories?" He smiled. "Maybe that's the point of what happened."

"Now you believe in the resurrection of the dead?"

"Why not?"

"You saw those bones out there in plastic bags. What is there to rise?"

"Reassembling bodies would be the least of it."

I tossed his notebook on the table. "Want some lunch?"

"Good. I'm starved."

That afternoon we filled the pool and, after a few unsuccessful attempts, got Ian's filter running. The temperature was in the high seventies and, though there was a breeze coming across the valley, we were shielded from it by the latticed fence Ian had built west of the pool area. Our conversation did not return to the topic raised inside. I made sure of that. I would have preferred an agnostic Connolly to the reborn Catholic he apparently was as the result of the crazy sequence of events at O'Hare. Memories of Newman Hall provided an inexhaustible source of safe talk, bringing back a time when we had seen eye to eye on everything. Inevitably Brady came up, and I couldn't resist saying that if he really wanted to make a splash, he should drop in on Brady out on the Via Nomentana.

"I'd rather make a splash in this pool."

And he did. He swam slowly the length of the pool and returned. He repeated this, again and again. When he finally came out, he collapsed into a chair, breathing heavily.

"I warned you about those cigarettes."

"What are my chances of retiring here?"

"Pretty good. The Wilsons like the idea of a live-in caretaker. That's how I came to be here."

He looked at me through half-closed eyes. "Honest Injun?"

"Of course you'd have to go public."

"Why?"

"Or you could go on pretending to be me. Not so easy with the Wilsons, since they know me."

He sat forward, hands on his knees, and looked around, at the pool and tennis courts, the house and the ruins of the abbey. "I really don't need anything this elaborate. Maybe I could buy a little place of my own."

"Using my credit cards?"

"I'll pay you back. I have money of my own. Quite a lot."

"Good for you. Write a check. Your bank will enjoy that."

"I predated one in Washington, and Nancy put it into her account and gave me some cash. I wonder if it cleared."

"It wouldn't work again. There's only one way you can get hold of your money. Well, maybe not just one. Who are your heirs?"

1 8 6

"I never made out a will."

"Shame. Do you have any relatives closer than Catherine?"

He shook his head. "If it goes to her, fine."

"You'll be a benefactor of the Carmelites."

"I've thought of that too."

So we were back on the topic I wanted to avoid. But only for a moment. I mentioned Horace's farm and Connolly was captivated. He became truly excited when I told him it was only miles away.

"Let's go see it."

"Tomorrow. I've got writing to do."

The medal around his neck swung when he turned to look at me. "I'll help you."

"The notebook will be a big help. I don't want to be hampered by facts."

"Don't continue with the biography, Jim."

"I have to eat."

"Write fiction."

"Maybe I am."

When I unpacked my bag in 8002 I found it was not mine. Same make, same color, but the contents were a stranger's. Had someone mistakenly taken my bag aboard that plane? I cannot remember any faces in that waiting room after I checked in for a flight bound for eternity. There is no identification on this bag, but it obviously belonged to someone younger than me. A corduroy sport coat, some washable pants, several turtlenecks. Just the costume for travel. By bus. They will not take cash at the rental-car counters, only credit cards. I cannot use my own, and I would not fly if I had cash enough for a ticket. I will go by bus. My manuscript went down with the plane. I feel free of all its tortured argument. The airport chaplain is curious about my presence at Mass. Today I said my own Mass in 8002 with bread from the coffee shop and burgundy obtained from room service, all the drapes drawn, using a leaflet missal from the underground chapel and the Gideon Bible for the readings. The chaplain and I are engaged in the same conspiracy, consecrating bread and wine here where planes take off and land with monotonous regularity. A few years ago priests said Mass defiantly with crackers and Coke. Who were they defying? I felt that I was reenacting my first Mass, though I said that in Latin. The Mass is always a reenactment. My breviary was in my bag. It is the only thing I would have wanted to salvage.

What have we all been up to since 1965? I suppose 1968 was the crucial year. I've been accused of trying to make Catholicism easy, and empty. My accusers are right. Even Clark, who claims to have lost his faith. How scandalized he looked in Rome when I told him about the sessions in the Palazzo della Cancelleria. Yet wasn't that the reaction I wanted? *Enfant terrible* saying terribly infantile things. Reciting the Creed at Mass, I savor the words as never before. Why did I want to twist and change them and make them say such odd things? To get a rise out of Clark? I pray for him. And for Nancy. Dear God. Blessed the man whose sins are forgiven.

When I told the chaplain I wanted to make a general confession he looked impatient, and when I said I was a priest he turned and stared at me. "What's your name?" I told him it didn't matter. What could he do but agree? He had no right to ask me that. He winced when I mentioned sins of the flesh. Adultery. I can believe he is a virgin.

So there it was, as clear an admission as I could expect. I felt a pain in my stomach that caused me to double over. Connolly and Nancy. It was as though I had never known before, not for sure, and had secretly hoped my suspicions were unfounded.

Chapter 2

The floor plan of Horace's house lay like a slightly elevated architectural drawing on a flat piece of ground overlooked by hills. In what had been the poet's bedroom, the mosaic floor, black and white tiles forming squares and diamonds, made a vivid impression on Connolly.

"*Exegi monumentum aere perennius,*" Connolly intoned. "Do you remember the rest?"

"I didn't remember that. This is where the old pagan screwed Lalage."

"I wonder if Benjie ever visited here?"

The Reverend Benjamin Hart, who had taught third-year Latin when we read Horace, was a short man with a florid face whose baldness suited his high domed head.

While we construed the assignment of the day, he would whip out a snow-white handkerchief and pat his brow with it, wring his hands, display the gamut of discontent at wooden renditions of the lines. Connolly managed to please him, I less so, but his own translations, delivered in a baritone, wakened in some of his students at least the sense that Horace could be more than a task. Connolly's translation of the *Ars Poetica* was printed in its entirety in the school magazine after receiving Benjie's imprimatur. I had countered with Catallus' lament for his dead brother, leaving the end in Latin: *Ave atque vale.* How recent all that seemed as we wandered through the two-dimensional rooms of Horace's house.

It was difficult not to wish that all the things that had happened since had not happened at all, particularly Nancy. Nancy and Connolly.

"The account of your general confession in the O'Hare chapel makes touching reading."

"Good God, I had forgotten I wrote about that."

"You were naughtier than I supposed."

"Who is Maria?"

"That's not the same thing."

"As what?"

I couldn't say it. If he had not kept the secret, I would. Again I felt a physical pain at the thought of Nancy betraying me with Connolly. He knew what I was thinking, I was sure of it. Before he might say what I would not, I stepped over the stones that outlined the rooms of Horace's house and started back to the car. Connolly caught up with me.

"We can eat in Tivoli," I said.

"I'm starved."

"You keep saying that."

"It keeps being true."

After pasta and veal and a shared liter of wine, we returned to the Abbadia Celestina, where Connolly noticed the crammed condition of the mailbox. Since I had been living incommunicado prior to his apparition out of the storm, I had not bothered about the Wilsons' mailbox. Now I emptied it and took the mail inside. There were, to my surprise, several letters for me, one from Cassell and another from Nancy. I managed to get them into my pocket before unlocking the door of the main house. I put the Wilsons' mail on the hall table and turned to find that Connolly had disappeared. He was in the living room, admiring the massive array of stereo equipment that Ian, who had a weakness for gadgetry and electronic doodads, had amassed.

"Is there a record collection?"

I opened the door of the small room in which Ian kept both his liquor and his record library. The latter would be the envy of many an FM station. *"Ecco,"* I said.

Connolly had followed me into the little room and began to examine the shelves and shelves of albums. I left him there, pleading the need to work, and went to the guest house.

Cassell's letter contained my semiannual royalty check, which was of reassuring size, not yet reflecting the dip in my fortunes. With it came a brief exhortation. "I am awaiting the Connolly MS eagerly and trust you are hard at work on it. Think of it as a rainy day book. I think it will make money and, who knows, soon the clouds will go away and the sun shine on other things as well." I had sent him two thousand dollars, his ten percent of the Furey advance, so he had a basis for thinking the biography of Connolly would bring in money. As for the rest of the note, well, I recognize whistling in the dark when I hear it. I opened Nancy's letter.

Dear Jim,

Michael is coming to see you, perhaps you have already seen him. If you have, you will now understand why I spoke to you as I did when we saw one another in Washington as well as in my last letter. But maybe you didn't get that letter, given the postal situation in Italy. I wish I were there with you. Remember all those years ago when the three of us were always together? Sometimes I think you should write a book about Michael after all. I don't know. If you could picture him the way he really is it could be an important book. I asked for books of yours at the library and they didn't have any, but then I remembered you use a pen name and the librarian suggested I look you up in *Contemporary Authors,* and there you were with all those names under which you write. So they did have lots of your books. I've read a couple of them and of course they're for kids, but I found them very well done. I wish we had talked of them when you were here, but of course it was not exactly a happy situation.

She went on, for pages, her memories of me always intertwined with memories of Connolly. I felt again as I had when Connolly's notebook removed any lingering doubt about the two of them. The final page of her letter had been written some days after the others, but it seemed the logical conclusion of what had gone before. She was going to try to change the time of her vacation so that she could come to Italy soon.

"There's someone in the pool."

Connolly showed no curiosity when I put Nancy's letter in my pocket.

He said, "I think it's Maria, the girl who's staying in your apartment in Rome."

Maria? My God. Connolly did not come with me when I left the guest house and headed for the pool. The sun was high and bright in the sky and, looking across the valley at the bluish haze softening the contours of hills and trees and buildings, I found my own thoughts to be similarly indistinct. Connolly had seemed a little peeved that our retreat had been invaded, though Maria had as much, or as little, right to show up unannounced as he did. But when I came around the poolside fence and saw Maria afloat on the greenish water, her body pale and surrealistic beneath the surface and her long hair tossing back and forth as she swam, I realized that I was angry she had come.

I walked around the pool to the point she was swimming toward and waited.

"Hi," she cried, dog paddling and looking up with a smile. Water beaded her round cheeks, and hair lay in spikes on her forehead. "Are you coming in?"

"When did you get here?"

"I don't have a watch."

There was charm in her assumption that her arrival could only be welcomed, but at the moment I was impervious to it. She came to the edge of the pool and reached up a hand.

"Help me out?"

She nearly pulled me in before I heaved her over the side. She rolled onto the hot tiles and began to laugh and it was difficult to ignore the memories her body evoked. She was wearing panties and a bra, which in their soaked condition were transparent.

"Why did you come here?"

She lay on her side and shielded her eyes with her hand. "Are you angry?"

Water puddled on the tiles in the shadow of her body. I knelt beside her. "Does Austin know you're here?"

"No!"

"Have you told him about this place?"

She sat up and hugged her knees to her breasts. Her anger now made us moral equals. "Why would you say a thing like that?"

I might have told her of the damage to the guest house. Until that moment I had been sure I was the victim of Ian's enemies in the village, but Maria's denial had been made with the anger of the guilty. It would be like her to have told Austin about the abbey. I turned and looked up toward the town, but it was the hill with its ravines and bushes and stunted trees that held my eye. Was Austin up there now, invisible, seeing everything, a malevolent presence more dangerous than Ian's infuriated neighbors? The once peaceful scene was now filled with menace. I had slept with the girl Austin considered his own and, worse, I had humiliated him in public in the street outside my building.

At the far end of the pool Maria's jeans and blouse were draped over a chair like signal flags at sea.

"How did you get here?"

"I took the bus."

"Get dressed."

"I want to swim." Her look was defiant but it was a child's look, a spoiled child's. I stood up.

"I'll get you a towel."

She was on her feet too, and again I found my eyes going over her body.

"Someone came calling for you. A man. That's why I came up."

"You already told me that. In Rome."

"Did he come here?"

"Maria, I came here to be alone. I'm trying to write a book."

"You're always writing a book."

"This is different."

She plunged into the pool and water splashed on me before I could get out of its way. When she came up, she cuffed her hand along the surface of the water and sent a spray to where I stood.

"Come on in."

How had I ever found her attractive? At the moment I wanted to take the long-handled rake with which the surface was cleared and flail her with it. I felt caught in the web of my past indiscretions. How many times did I have to learn that there are no casual affairs before the lesson took? There is no free lunch nor free love either. One always pays a higher price than he counted on. Maria would not disappear simply because I had tired of her. She had been out of my mind for weeks. But my indifference seemed to claim her more than my middle-aged possessiveness had done. Once I had even been jealous of her. I looked again at the looming hill. If Austin was up there, if I could see him, I would have shouted for him to come down and take Maria away. But he was no more likely to be the instrument of my wishes than Maria.

Concupiscence is a feckless ally. Maria's legs scissored as she crossed the pool and I stepped out of my wet trousers, pulled off my sweater, and dove in. If anger and indifference did not work, perhaps a facsimile of my former lovesick self would alter her attitude.

I swam swiftly to where she waited in the center of the pool, alerted by the sound of my dive. Facing her, working my arms and legs easily, I leaned forward and kissed her chlorined lips.

"Some welcome," she said.

"You surprised me."

"That was the idea."

"Well, it worked. My writing isn't going well."

"Poor Jimmy."

"Poor is the right word. If this book isn't successful, that is what I will be." I knew talk of money bored her.

"Tell me about it." Her lips were colorless and her wet lashes gave her a startled look. Had she removed her contacts?

"You wouldn't like it. It's a fantasy."

"For kids?"

"Of all ages."

"Let me read what you've done."

She had never shown the least curiosity about my literary products. That had been one of her charms. Now, like Nancy, she was interested in my career when it was on the downgrade.

"What I would like is some time off. Let's go back to Rome."

"And leave this place? Why? It's perfect here."

"I've been here too long. I'm bored with it."

"Well I just got here."

"We can come back later."

"Promise?"

I was no more anxious for her to meet Connolly than he seemed to be to meet her. As we bobbed about in the pool, my mind searched for a way to get Maria out of there while at the same time alerting Connolly that we were going. I could not simply disappear. And then I remembered the telephone. I kissed Maria and thought of Wilde. The coward does it with a kiss.

"Enjoy your swim. I'll put some things together and we'll leave."

"Jimmy, I don't want to leave."

"I don't mean right away."

"It'll be dark when we get back to Rome."

"I'm counting on that."

Her look became sly. "We don't have to go all the way to Rome for that."

"You're right. How would you like to spend the night in Tivoli?"

"I'd rather stay here."

"Not tonight."

She cocked her head and shut one eye. "You act as if you have someone else here."

"I do."

Her mouth opened. I came close to her and whispered. "The ghosts of the monks."

Beneath the water she entwined her legs in mine and brought her body close against me. The thought of a night with her no longer seemed merely a trick to get her away from the Abbadia Celestina.

"Don't go away," I said.

I swam for the ladder and pulled myself up into the now chilling air. Maria watched as I pulled my trousers over my wet underwear, then turned on her back and floated. When I was out of sight of the pool, I ran toward the main house.

I rang the guest house and waited patiently, wondering if Connolly was there and if he would answer the phone.

"*Pronto?*"

"Michael, this is Jim. Look, I'm going to take her back to Rome. It's the only way to get rid of her."

"She's already seen me. In Rome."

"I'm afraid she might have led her boyfriend here."

"Her boyfriend?"

"It's a long story."

"What if the people who own the place show up while you're gone?"

"They won't. They're in England."

"How long will you be gone?"

"I'm not sure. I'll phone you."

"You're taking the car?"

"There's plenty to eat. You'll be okay."

"Would it be all right if I listen to music over there?"

"Michael, you can do anything you want."

"I'll stay out of sight until you're gone."

"Fine."

"I appreciate what you're doing."

I looked at the phone after I put it down. What did he think I was doing? Connolly was proving to be a shy Lazarus, hiding out in the O'Hare Hilton, going by bus to Washington and assuming my identity and credit cards in order to come to Rome. His impulse had been to seek out first Nancy and now me. Was he, like Nancy in her letter, in the grip of nostalgia for the days when they had deceived me? Well, if I was protecting anyone, it was myself. I could not rid myself of the thought that Maria, in a mindlessly spiteful moment, had told Austin of the abbey, and had stoked anew the rage of a boy she herself considered mad. Nor was it easy to forget how he had threatened me on the phone.

And there was something else. To appear before Connolly in the company of the clinging Maria would kick a major prop from under my self-esteem. For years I had been, in my own eyes, the injured party, betrayed by my wife and Connolly. I did not want to become a foolish figure in the eyes of either of them.

But was it any less foolish to become an accomplice of Connolly's feigned death?

It was more difficult to get Maria out of the house than it had been to get her out of the pool. She wandered through the rooms with a delighted expression, obviously enthralled. In the living room, she opened double doors and went out onto the terrace. I did not try to stop her. She was on the side of the house opposite the guest house. On a table, glasses still stood from when Connolly and I had drinks there.

Maria looked back at me. "Is there some Cinzano? I'd like a drink."

"We'll have a drink in Tivoli."

She came to me, eyes downcast, and put a hand on my chest. "Let's stay here."

"After I've had a little vacation from it. This house has become a prison."

"Show me where you work."

"I work everywhere. In the dining room, here on the terrace, down by the pool."

"I meant it when I said I'd like to read what you've written."

"I've got a long way to go before I have anything readable."

"What's upstairs?" She pressed by me into the living room.

"More rooms."

"I want to see."

She had put on her jeans but not her blouse. Now she turned to me, her hands behind her back, and unhooked her brassiere. I put my arms around her and she pressed against me.

"Show me the upstairs."

We made love in the room where I had slept the night Connolly appeared. It was a stupid thing to do, but when had I ever done anything that was not stupid? Connolly, in the guest house, must have wondered why we were taking so long to leave. It seemed an act of defiance to delay our departure, particularly since he had assumed my motive in going was to protect him from discovery. Maria's indifference to him seemed total. A man supposedly dead had come asking for me and this had made no impression on her at all. But if I was acting at least partly from defiance, her act of passion was clearly designed to drive Tivoli from my mind. I was content to benefit from her deception. Our delay in going made Connolly a prisoner in the guest house. It seemed time that he should suffer at least some inconvenience for the hoax he had begun to perpetrate at O'Hare.

"Tell me about the man who didn't die." Maria lay on her side, a pillow tucked between shoulder and chin, looking at me with nearsighted eyes. Her contact lenses were in a plastic case in her purse. They might have been scales removed, explaining her delayed curiosity.

"I am a man and I didn't die."

"The one who came asking for you."

"You tell me. You saw him."

"I described him for you. Your not quite identical twin."

"Weren't you wearing glasses then either?"

She wore her nails long and now punched at my chest with her index finger. "You said he was your friend Connolly."

"No. You told me the man called himself Connolly. But Connolly is dead."

She shrugged and began to erase with the ball of her finger the indentation made by her nail. "Get us a drink, Jimmy."

The setting sun was red in the west. To make love after swimming and after the trip to Horace's house made me less eager to get her out of there. It was in Connolly's interest to stay out of sight. Why should I accommodate him further than I already had by taking Maria to the main house?

"What would you like?"

"Surprise me."

I surprised her with brandy and we settled back in bed, side by side, resting our glasses on our sheeted stomachs.

"How could you get bored with this place."

"It gets lonely."

She made a throaty sound and put her hand beneath the sheet. Poor forked animal, Swift called man. It is a better definition than rational animal. Maria sought and found the organ of decision. To hell with Tivoli.

Much later, waking in the now-dark room, Maria a fetal ball asleep beside me, I listened to the strangely audible night outside, the sough of cicadas, remote rumors of traffic and the barking of a dog. Country dogs do bay at the moon. Sleep had cleared my head of brandy but not my limbs of lassitude. I was very hungry, but I accepted the fact as I would a headache, an affliction that would pass with time. Close by, undecodable sounds took on significance from being attended to. Had the sounds been there when I was not awake to hear them? Perhaps they had wakened me. I lifted my head slightly from the pillow and listened intently. Small snaps and scrapings, a branch rustling against the house, night birds, crawling things—there was a whole world out there to be constructed by imagination since I had no knowledge of the beasts and birds that prey by night.

A sudden soft plosive sound not far enough away made me get out of bed. On the way to the window, I collided with a chair and stopped like a frozen film, holding my breath. Maria stirred but did not waken. From the window I looked out at the ruins of the abbey, visible in the milky light of the moon. As I stood there its visibility increased, as if some handle were being slowly turned offstage. And then I saw Connolly.

In that light he seemed ghost indeed, standing in the apse of the abbey church. He stooped as I watched him, and I could see him lift the plywood cover over the crypt where those bags of bones were buried. Had he lifted and then lost his grip on that cover before? He straightened and assumed a motionless pose, his head bowed. He might have been praying for the dead monks become now only a grayish detritus of bone. Any Mass he celebrated contained a commemoration of the departed which would have included those monks, but the sight of him standing silently at night in the ruins of the church where they too once had prayed suggested a physical as well as temporal continuity between Michael Connolly, priest, and his long-dead brethren.

The dark night of the soul, a phrase comprising the temptation to doubt, seemed conducive to faith, or at least to the memory of it. Centuries from now would some priest come from afar pray among the ruins of Newman Hall for Connolly and me? Whatever bones were unearthed there would belong to neither him nor me. Whose corpse had been buried near that island chapel a few weeks ago? Perhaps those of the man who had mistakenly carried Connolly's bag onto the doomed flight to Washington.

In his notebook, Connolly had thanked God for sparing his life. Plato once pondered the ignorance of survivors who thank their rescuer. How do they know what future terrors await them? Perhaps evils worse than the shipwreck they had lived to tell about. What future, immediate or remote, did Connolly imagine he was saved for? His present inclination seemed to be to stay here at Abbadia Celestina and continue the retreat begun at the O'Hare Hilton. I would have liked a cigarette, but apart from the fact that it might waken Maria, it would alert Connolly to the fact that he was being watched. Was it possible that he thought Maria and I had gone to Rome?

The noise that had brought me from my bed came again. Connolly had let drop the plywood cover of the crypt. He certainly was not behaving as if he might disturb anyone asleep in the house. He began to walk, going down a little flight of steps to the cloister. The patterned brick of the cloister walks had emerged from the rubble of time intact. The sprinkling system Ian had attached to the cloister well could be turned on from the house, and the thought of dowsing Connolly gave me a brief boyish delight.

At Newman Hall, as a year's end prank, Connolly had played a firehose over the quad from a window in the college corridor, a great arc of water like a liquid rainbow that bombarded the windows of the rector's apartment. Luckily Brady's windows were shut. Luckily, too, the next day was the start of summer vacation. Connolly had usually timed his antics well in those days. Now he paced the cloister walk of the Abbadia Celestina as Father Black had paced the study hall saying his breviary, lips moving, brow nettled at the sound of boys at their books. Over lunch in Tivoli that day, Connolly and I had reminisced as if we were a two-man alumni club, products of a school that no longer existed.

"Even if it did it wouldn't be the same, Jim. The major seminary is nothing like it was."

"Ah, Vatican II."

He sipped his mineral water and looked across the square where a row of hopeful taxis waited to take tourists back to Rome for an exorbitant fee, but a fee they were often willing to pay rather than face the prospect of returning in the buses that had brought them. "Seminarians are largely a fey bunch now. I've heard so much talk of homosexuality."

I had heard the same stories. "I prefer to hear they go out on dates."

"They have regular dances at a Dominican novitiate near Chicago."

"Boccaccio."

"And the nuns." He made a face and shook his head. "Catherine won't listen to stories about that."

"Thank God for the Carmelites."

He looked at me curiously. "That's an old remark from an apostate."

"I also approve of the Vestal Virgins."

"Have you really lost your faith?"

"Have you really rediscovered yours?"

The way he lifted his glass was almost liturgical. He looked me in the eye when he nodded. "That is the way I think of it too."

"Spared by the hand of God?"

"How would you describe it?"

"A happy accident. A comedy of errors. And then a not very funny hoax."

"I'm deceiving no one."

"You're deceiving everyone."

He shook the suggestion away. "Call it chance. But why chance? Why those accidents just then?" He put down his glass. "It's my fault, isn't it?"

"Chance?"

"Your loss of faith."

Over his shoulder I could see a shaded stand where tourists, finished with their lunch, were examining souvenirs, leather boxes from Florence, imitation Renaissance globes, various onyx items. I did not want to hear from his own lips the confession of his betrayal. That would have been yet another deed of treachery, involving as it did Nancy. He had no right to confess her sins to me.

"Is that your explanation of what happened? You were spared to bring me back into the fold?"

"And myself too."

"You recant all your exciting theological innovations?"

"That is the easiest part of all."

204

"Are reactionaries made so easily? Next you'll be telling me the Council was a mistake."

"Of course not. My writings had little to do with the Council."

"You must have a chat with Furey. He would love you in your new incarnation. You can write your autobiography for him and live happily ever after."

"What sort of book is he expecting from you?"

"I told you. A portrait of a heretic."

He smiled. "There's not much to choose between him and the theologian I was."

"When will you rise from the dead?"

"The same day you will."

In the car going back he asked me if I had ever read Camus's *La Chute*. "The narrator is Jean-Baptiste Clamence, and he is a judge penitent. I am a penitent theologian. That seems to be the way to make amends. What good would yet another public declaration from me do? I know what I would have said of someone like myself who did that. I had professional protection against such things. No. I'm content to wait for the general resurrection."

"You'll have to go through another funeral first."

"Yes."

"In the meantime you could end your days in some unruined monastery."

"I would have to explain things to get in. It would all come out. I really don't think that would serve any good purpose."

He had met a Little Brother of Jesus in Rome, a follower of Charles Foucauld, and he thought he might mimic that life in a free-lance sort of way, a worker priest aswim in the sea of the people. It was on that drive that I knew, twenty thousand dollars or not, that I would stop work on his life. Hagiography had never appealed to me, and it was clear that Connolly was belatedly seeking sanctity rather than renown.

I got back into bed without waking Maria and, lying on my back, was prepared for insomnia, but sleep came quickly.

I seldom dream but I dreamed then, a mad jumble of images obeying no chronology of the waking world: Vietnam, Newman Hall, the first days of my marriage to Nancy. In the land of dreams a marriage is never annulled. Chance might have brought Nancy and me together, but, like Connolly, I did not then really believe in chance. What I remembered was New York and the three of us together, Nancy and Greg and myself. I dreamed I cried, perhaps I really did. I had no defense against the sadness of that loss. In the logic of the unleashed mind, life seemed a tale of loss, and every good thing I had ever known receded from me as I lifted like a spaceship into the void.

The sound of music awoke me. It was still dark at the windows, no hint of dawn. Maria was not in bed beside me. This time when I got up I dressed. The volume on the stereo was set high, and I wondered if Connolly could hear the music in the guest house. At the window I checked the abbey, but there was no sign of him there. Surely he had gone to bed by now. My impatience with Maria returned, but when I came into the upper sitting room where Connolly and I had talked before the fire I realized that the music I was hearing was not the kind Maria favored.

I went slowly down the stone staircase, and before I reached the bottom I heard their voices.

Maria, wrapped in a robe of Ian's, sat in a chair sipping from a cup. Connolly was dressed as he had been when I saw him wandering about the moonlit ruins of the abbey. He sat across from her smoking a cigarette.

"I had a sandwich," Maria said when she noticed me. "Aren't you starved?"

Connolly got to his feet. "I didn't realize you were still here. Sorry about the music."

"It's better than an alarm clock," I said, avoiding his eyes. "What kind of sandwich did you have?"

"Some kind of salami sliced as thin as paper."

She did not offer to make a sandwich for me. Why should she? I asked Connolly if he was hungry.

"Do ghosts eat?" Maria asked.

"Only by the full moon."

Connolly came with me into the kitchen and repeated his apology for the stereo. But his real regret was that Maria had seen him again. "How much does she know?"

"She can read and write and count up to a hundred or so."

"You know what I mean."

"She was with me the day I learned of the plane crash and decided to go home for your funeral."

"Why did you do that, Jim?"

"Why not?"

"You're a morbid Irishman, and you know it. I'm touched."

"I wanted to see Nancy."

He had nothing to say to that, thank God. Perhaps Maria's presence stifled the confessional mood he had fleetingly felt in Tivoli over lunch. The Wilsons' refrigerator contained only a little cheese but its freezer was full of meat, and in the pantry were bottles of the wine Ian had made from grapes grown on his land. Connolly cut himself a piece of cheese and accepted the offer of a glass of wine when I told him its origin.

"Living off the land," he said.

"With Ian it's a gentleman's hobby. Maybe that's one reason the natives resent him."

"I find it difficult to have a conversation with Maria."

"So do I."

Another possible line of conversation cut off. He could not fail to realize that we had been together upstairs. Maria's animal contentment as she ate her sandwich was unmistakable, at least to me. Connolly should recognize it from his experience with Nancy. I looked at him with sudden hatred.

"Who is Austin, Jim?"

"Who did Maria say he was?"

"That was unclear."

"A boy."

"Did he really threaten to kill you?"

"Have some more cheese." I handed him the knife as if I were getting rid of a weapon.

"Do you plan to marry her?"

"No."

"Why not?"

"I would need reasons for it, not the absence of reasons against it. Maybe I will propose to Nancy again. Now that she's free."

He looked at me and it was difficult to know what he was thinking.

I said, "You could officiate again."

"Maria seems to misunderstand your intentions."

"Does she? I doubt it. She is an example of the new woman. Don't think of her as a defenseless maiden."

I took my sandwich and wine into the other room where Maria, her head cocked to one side, was attending to the music. "Is that the only kind of record here?"

"You're hearing Liszt," Connolly told her. "The Hungarian Rhapsodies."

Maria was unimpressed. Nor was I in the mood for a musical soiree. It was now two in the morning. When the piece ended and in the silence another record plunked onto the turntable, Connolly offered to turn it off. Neither Maria nor I said the polite thing. He turned the stereo off. Silence seemed to creep out of the corners of the room and enfold us. The telephone rang.

Maria and I were seated, and Connolly, who was on his feet, looked at the ringing phone as if he had never seen one before.

"Don't answer it," I said.

"Austin doesn't know I'm here," Maria said with insistence.

"He'd better not." But again I was sure she was lying.

The phone continued to ring, becoming more shrill as it did so. Finally Connolly picked it up. He listened after saying *Pronto* and then covered the mouthpiece with his hand. "It's long distance. Nancy wants to speak with you."

"I'm not here."

"Of course you're here."

"Talk to her if you want to."

"Your wife?" Maria mouthed rather than spoke these words, her eyes wide with I know not what emotion.

"I have no wife."

"Hello, Nancy," Connolly said into the phone, beckoning me to come.

It would be difficult to imagine worse circumstances in which to talk with her. Connolly crossed the room after he had handed me the phone, but Maria did not even pretend not to listen to the conversation, or at least to my end of it.

"Who was that who answered?"

"Nancy, it is two in the morning here."

"It was Michael, wasn't it?"

"I got your letter."

"Good. That's why I'm calling. I leave tomorrow night. I arrive in Rome the following morning. Could you possibly meet my flight?"

"All right. Give me the number and time."

After she did, she said. "Have you talked with Michael?"

"That would be difficult."

"Haven't you seen him?"

"Don't be silly." If Connolly wanted to play dead I would be his accomplice.

"Jimmy, I know he answered the phone."

"I'll meet your flight."

"We can all talk together."

"Do you tell fortunes too?"

"Please."

"That's my aim."

"You sound so close."

"So do you."

I wished I were alone, out of earshot, but what would I have said if I were? Marriage has its pains, but annulment has no pleasures. Wary and waiflike, Maria watched me. I winked at her and had the absurd thought that Nancy knew I had. I repeated that I would meet her plane and then it was over.

"She's coming to Rome," Maria said.

I nodded.

"I want to meet her."

"Why not?"

"Do you mean it?"

I smiled what was meant to be a mysterious smile.

Connolly said, "When is she coming?"

"The day after tomorrow."

"Here."

"You heard me. I will pick her up at the airport."

"And I'll come with you," Maria said, rising from her chair.

She came to me, took my glass, and drank the rest of my wine. Moist lips, sparkling puffy eyes, tousled hair. What a trio we made. A man thought dead, a wanton girl, and a failed writer for boys. The prospect of Nancy's arrival seemed to fit all too well into the crazy scramble my life had become. Why did I feel guilty when it was Nancy who had deceived me and had our marriage annulled, Connolly who was perpetrating a hoax, and Maria who had come uninvited to my mountain retreat? I had every right to feel the victim. But something like the memory of remorse sat like pasta in my stomach, digesting me rather than the reverse.

Connolly seemed to want to say something but was disinclined to do so in the presence of Maria. I suggested that it had been a long day, and Connolly left somewhat reluctantly for the guest house. In the kitchen, Maria refilled the glass she had taken from me and bore it like a libation up the stairs and back to bed.

Chapter 3

I rose before seven the following morning. Maria moaned and rolled away, pulling the covers tightly about her. Let her sleep. I went over to the guest house where Connolly had just finished saying his Mass on the refectory table.

"Bless you," he said when I told him I wanted to work. "You always were a methodical devil."

"I should have been a Methodist."

"You would have died of thirst."

He took his O'Hare notebook and an apple and went outside. Seated at the table, I could see him as he walked out to the abbey, settled on a bench, opened his notebook, and began to write. I pushed away the pages of the biography and put a clean piece of paper in my typewriter.

The body of Becky Callahan was discovered by a pair of lovers who had carried their blanket and picnic basket from a car parked on the shoulder of the country road. Their intended springtime idyll was aborted when they came upon the woman lying face down among last autumn's leaves, left like them to rot unseen. One arm of the corpse was extended and in its open palm was a Kennedy half-dollar.

I stared at that opening and tried to imagine the mystery novel that would follow it. Furey's money would have to be returned. Cassell would be furious and probably urge me to let Furey think I meant to fulfill my promise until I proved I could succeed in another fiction genre. No contract of the usual sort had been drawn up, the check Furey had written was a personal one, the whole thing was what is somewhat mysteriously called a gentlemen's agreement. Cassell's imagined casuistic argument was obvious. The money could be viewed as a wealthy man's subvention of an author momentarily down on his luck. Furey could afford to be a patron of the arts, if the product of my typewriter deserved so lofty a designation. But keeping the money would link me in some mystical way to the Michael Connolly who had escaped death in a plane crash and now regarded himself in an altered light.

He sat in the morning sun writing with the diligence of a schoolboy in the spiral notebook he had bought in a Carson, Pirie, Scott outlet at O'Hare, and I wondered what further confidences he was addressing to whatever reader we imagine when we pretend to be writing to ourselves. One writes to discover what one thinks, trying to put some order into the chaos of the mind. Connolly, the self-described theologian, fresh from saying Mass, sat among the memories of medieval monks laying bare his soul to the God those monks had praised in this place centuries before.

Why did I resent what seemed to be his genuine conversion? In his dissident days I had been his severest critic. I was the champion of the simple faith I had lost: let believers accept blindly what has been revealed. I should be delighted by his return to docility, but I was not. On the assumptions of the faith I had lost, Connolly as penitent was a likely candidate for bliss hereafter. Perhaps I bridled at the scarcely conscious thought that he would best me in the ultimate sweepstakes and that from the spot in hell reserved for apostates I must for all eternity watch Michael Connolly cavorting with his God.

I shifted my typewriter to the end of the table where I could work without looking out the window and went back to my mystery. A mystery, I decided, is best kept a mystery from its author, at least while it is being written. A swarm of possible murderers of Becky Callahan came to mind, a life constructed itself, an improbable plot formed in my mind and the background crept with menace. What I was writing began to seem reasonably like the mysteries I had read, and I pounded away at my typewriter in that special flush of excitement which comes when one has found his path.

Writing, like doing crossword puzzles, is absorbing work. Three hours passed and I had written seven pages before I pushed away from my typewriter, willing to call it a day. I was now convinced that I could go on with the story I had begun.

At the window, I looked out and saw Maria and Connolly in conversation. He had come down from the abbey ruins, and they were in lawn chairs under the shadow of the tower. Last night he had said Maria was difficult to have a conversation with. He did not seem to be having any difficulty now. I could imagine what she might say to him, but what would Michael Connolly say to Maria? His notebook was on the grass beside his chair. I doubted that he would discuss with Maria the sort of thing he wrote in it. I took a bottle of beer from the refrigerator and went outside to join them.

A silence fell as I approached, and I felt like an intruder.

"I could hear the tapping of your typewriter," Connolly said. His hand dropped from the arm of his chair to the notebook lying on the grass.

"You're still writing in that?"

"I'm still on retreat."

There were just the two lawn chairs there, though others could be brought from the terrace. I sat on the grass and, in response to Maria's waggling fingers, gave her the bottle of beer. She had one bronzed leg crossed over the other and moved a stubby-toed foot back and forth. Her public body seemed a foreign object, and it took an effort to imagine us in bed together the night before.

"Tomorrow your wife comes," she said.

"Yes."

"When will you start for Rome?"

"We can leave in the morning."

"You're sure it will be all right if I come along?"

"It was your idea."

"I've been having second thoughts."

"Don't be silly."

I wanted to get her away from the abbey, back to Rome, out of my life. The previous night had been as much routine as passion. How weary of her I was. What had she and Connolly been discussing? The feeling that I was intruding persisted, and I wondered if he had been offering her spiritual counsel. That was how he had started with Nancy, the priest who subsequently became a lover. Attempting to see Maria through his eyes, I saw a vacant-headed girl enormously attractive on the level of the least common denominator between male and female. But Connolly had refound his faith and his mind should be on higher things. Do repentant theologians succumb to temptations of the flesh?

Connolly stretched and put back his head in a yawn. Then he excused himself and got to his feet.

"I am going to take a nap."

"And I am going to the pool," Maria said, handing me what was left of the beer.

I was dying to talk about my successful morning's work but repressed the impulse. It is lethal to discuss work in progress. Not that I had ever had much opportunity to do that. Cassell saw my books as commodities and was little interested in what went into the making of them. Connolly walked slowly to the house while Maria and I remained on the lawn.

"Have a good talk?" I asked.

"He's easy to talk to."

"Did you confess your sins?"

"What sins?"

It might have been a joke, you never know with Maria. Once she had answered "Where else?" when I told her she was undersexed. But she was sincere now, I was sure of it. She belonged to a generation that has no sense of sin or remorse. Confession has become the sacrament of reconciliation, priests become counselors rather than confessors. She had never known the anguished wait before the grille opened and in a strangled voice one recounted a list of mortal sins, scraping at the acoustical wallboard of the little box with nervous nails, dreading the jeremiad that would come from the priest when he learned the extent of one's turpitude.

"What did you talk about?"

"Nothing. Everything. He just listens."

"I hope you didn't divulge all our secrets."

She stretched her lips in disapproval. "He doesn't care about that."

2 1 6

"How do you know?"

"I just know."

I let it go. Eventually Maria would tell me about it, if it struck her as important. But what future was I thinking of in which she might tell me of her talk with Connolly? I wanted to be rid of her and to keep her both. What I really wanted, of course, was to have her without strings, and I knew that was impossible. Had she again told Connolly that we were going to marry? I got off the grass and settled into the chair Connolly had vacated.

Maria lifted her legs and held them straight out before her while at the same time leaning forward and extending her arms. Her only contact with the chair was her bottom. She might have been levitating as Furey's Margaret Rusher was wont to do. Her bodily attitude made her breasts more prominent and her face in profile looked less unformed and childlike. Did she really imagine that we would marry? Annulment or no annulment, I still felt married to Nancy. What God had put together not even the archdiocesan marriage court of Washington, D.C., could put asunder.

Maria's feet dropped to the grass and she rose in a single fluid motion, levering herself erect.

"Are you coming in?"

"Maybe later."

She nodded and walked diagonally across the lawn toward the pool. Her body had womanly authority, canceling her youth, and I watched her out of sight as the elders had watched Susanna.

I picked up Connolly's notebook, put it in my lap and opened it.

The summer before my last year at Newman Hall I visited the Trappist monastery of New Mount Melleray outside Dubuque, and there was a diocesan priest living in the guest house who had skipped out of his parish and done God knows what and then come back and his bishop had sent him to the Trappists as a punishment. He was middle-aged, white-haired, flushed complexion, probably a drinker. He wore loafers and a sheepish look and avoided me after he found out I was a seminarian. The spring before I had read *Shepherds in the Mist* and been both fascinated and scandalized by its accounts of renegade priests. That odd little man in the guest house did not strike me as a tragic or romantic figure, just weak. I wondered if he had come back out of repentance or because he missed the settled security of clerical life. Whatever happened to him? Today he would not even raise an eyebrow; he would be described as on leave and remain on the payroll. Is it possible to assign myself the penance his bishop gave him? This ruined abbey is what I have been seeking since I left O'Hare. I want to make amends for what I have been and done and written, and this is an ideal place for that. All along I have craved anonymity without knowing it. All the noisy recognition when I was out on the lecture circuit, object of the awed admiring look celebrities get, was corrupting. Would there be any dissident theology without the media? Movie stars sometimes say they envy those who can travel unnoticed; the fame they sought has become a nuisance. I never really felt that until I heard in 8002 that the plane had crashed and knew I was free of the persona I had become. B. Traven. Ambrose Bierce gone off to Mexico and never heard from again. I must get beyond the phony and romantic. It is hard not to see what has happened, and what I have done, as Clark does—a hoax or game which will end when I burst into a TV studio crying, Here I am. Surprise, surprise. But a self-imposed penance lies lightly on the shoulders. When Newman returned to England from Italy, the voyage when he composed "Lead Kindly Light," he had the persistent feeling that God had a work for him to do. That is how I feel now. I was preserved for some purpose. Clark thought I meant I was snatched from the jaws of death to nag him back to belief. He flatters himself that he has become an unbeliever. He could as easily lose his memory, his outlook, his grim Irish way of seeing the world as a Vale of

Tears. He kicks against the goad and that is all. How pathetic his liaison with the girl Maria. She is a lovely little drone convinced that life has dealt unfairly with her. Unfairly! I sit here in the sun near the bones of my unknown departed brethren and invoke their prayers that I might know what it is I am meant to do. Did I ever think of my writing and lecturing as a vocation? I do not think I have had an interior life since I left the seminary. Catherine conveys the same judgment without putting it into words. Carmelites know how to communicate with silence.

This entry, like the others I had read, presumed that life is a story and that Connolly must get clear on the meaning of his. When men lose faith in immortality, they transfer their thirst for meaning to the race, as if mankind were going somewhere, as if history has a beginning, a middle and an end. But each man dies and the race is doomed and there will be no spectator when the curtain is rung down at last, so where is the meaning?

When Connolly began to play fast and loose with the dogma of the Resurrection, he had to see doctrine as evolving. But that put meaning in some indefinite future. What good is that to the present generation?

Vale of tears. Connolly was wrong to use that phrase of me. *In hac lacrimarum valle*—but the valley leads to uplands where tears are dried and joy complete. Tears suggest a contrast. Where was I to find one unless, like Connolly, I took up again the faith of our common upbringing? The only substitute I had was the tidy arrangement of imagined incidents in fiction.

I took Connolly's notebook back to the guest house and put it on the refectory table. He was napping in the main house, Maria was in the pool. And I was hungry. I decided to surprise them with a plate of sandwiches. We could eat beside the pool.

Chapter 4

From the back stoop, in peripheral vision, I saw an object on the road. I turned, but there was nothing save the afterimage of a man. I ran across the gravel path, leapt over the small creek, and started up the incline to where I would reach the road. My footsteps on the gravel seemed to send out signals of warning to the intruder, but once I was on the hill I moved in silence. It was difficult to keep my footing. Twice I slipped and prevented myself from sliding down only by taking large handfuls of weeds. I came to the edge of the road at last and, keeping to the side, to muffle my passage, walked stealthily toward the public road.

Where the road turned, bringing the stone gate posts

into view, I again looked at nothing. My eye went up the steeper hill to the town, but there was no one visible on it. Where had he gone? I decided to go back.

In the main house, before going upstairs, I looked out at Maria. Lying face down on spread-out towels, eyes closed, she was a picture of indolent security. Connolly was not asleep.

"We've got to get out of here," I said.

"What's wrong?"

"I just saw Austin. He was on the road when I came out of the guest house."

"So?"

"He's crazy. He's the boy who wants to kill me. I have to get Maria away from here quick."

He sat up on the bed and put his feet on the floor. "Go ahead. There's no reason for me to leave."

"I think we should all get out of here. Remember what he did to the guest house."

"You don't know that was the boy."

His point seemed pedantic. I might just as well doubt that I had seen Austin on the road. "Yes, I do."

Connolly got his feet into the slippers he had borrowed from Ian's closet. "It will be better if I stay. You two leave and I'll stay here. If I get the stereo going and make the place look inhabited, you'll have a better chance of getting away from him."

"Mike, he's dangerous."

"He has nothing against me."

"He had nothing against the guest house either."

"Except that you were staying there."

He wanted to help me get Maria out of there, but equally he did not want to leave himself. Nonetheless, his idea seemed a good one. Maria and I could go back around the abbey, down into the vineyard and make our way, concealed by the vines, into the valley. By the time we were visible we would be miles away. All the same, I wished there was some way we could leave in the car without passing the point where I had seen Austin. But no way occurred to me.

Downstairs, Connolly turned on the stereo to deafening volume, wincing as he did so. He had found the sort of hard rock Maria likes. "I can't stay in this house with that on. Let's change shirts. I'll go over to the guest house, facing away from the road, and he might mistake me for you."

I pulled off my flannel shirt and Connolly gave me his sweat shirt. It was gray, with Notre Dame in large blue letters across the chest. The rock music on the stereo had to be audible in the town above. Connolly went to the front door, opened it and turned.

"Will you bring Nancy with you when you come back?"

"Why not? You already appeared to her."

"And you're the only one she told."

Was that a statement or a question? Either way, it had the effect of binding the three of us together in a way I did not like. Connolly stepped outside, pulled the door behind him and was gone.

At the pool, I put my foot gently in the small of Maria's back and jostled her. A smile formed on her lips but her eyes did not open. "Mmmmm."

"Maria, we're leaving."

She rolled on her back and squinted up at me. "You said tomorrow."

"I've changed my mind. Get into your clothes." Her swimming attire was still panties and bra.

"Why is the stereo on so loud?" Music rolled from the house, assaulting the mountain air. Pulsating rhythm, repetitive lyrics produced by tone-deaf illiterates with a strange designation: The End of the World.

"Connolly is testing the equipment."

"He'll burn out the speakers."

She had one foot in her jeans when she lost her balance and came hopping toward me. I steadied her and she slipped into the other leg. "Why are we going?"

"I want to do some things in Rome before meeting Nancy's plane."

"Like get rid of me?"

"Maybe."

"But you said I could meet her."

"I didn't mean meet her plane."

"Then when?"

"She'll be staying for a while. Don't worry about it."

"I'm not worried."

I was. With Austin lurking about there was no peace in the country house. He was the one I wanted to lure back to Rome, though only after Maria and I got a head start. The Wilson place was too vulnerable to the kind of irrationality Austin was capable of. Maria balked when I started toward the abbey.

"I thought we were leaving."

"We are."

"The car is on the other side of the house."

"We're not taking the car. I don't want Connolly to be stranded here."

"Then he can take us to Tivoli and the bus."

"It will be a nice walk."

"You're kidding."

"Come on." I took her hand and smiled invitingly. "You've never gone this way."

She didn't like it, but it would have been a mistake to tell her our reason for leaving, although mention of Austin might have made her willing enough to take the hike she had trouble seeing as a romantic lark. But she came along.

At the point where steps led up to the abbey, another

flight led down to a grassy plateau that ringed the flattened hill on which the monastery had been built. We followed this around and, behind the abbey, I started downhill to the vineyard.

"Where in hell are we going?" Maria demanded.

I pointed beyond the vineyard to a tobacco field and, farther off, a white dusty road.

"But how far is Tivoli?"

"On a day like this, who cares?" I squeezed her hand but she did not squeeze back.

If she was reluctant at the outset, her lack of enthusiasm increased as we went between the rows of the vineyard, the vines twisted grotesquely on frames so that a row seemed one continuous growth. New leaves were out and, if it had not been for the dusty shifting soil, it could have been a pleasant walk. Music from the house followed us as we went and it seemed an added incentive to go. When I stopped to look back, I was struck by how unfamiliar the Wilson place looked from that angle. We were on a much lower level now, and the bulk of the ruined abbey concealed both the house and much of the hill beyond it. Civitella was more visible, and I saw a car going up the narrow twisting road that led to it. The campanile whose bell tolled across the valley could be seen, and the huddle of houses making one choppy outline against the sky. Maria shook dirt from her tennis shoes and glared at me.

"This is crazy."

"I know."

"How can you smile like that?"

"I have gas on my stomach."

By the time we came out of the vineyard we had reached a point where going back was as unappealing as going on. Maria, sullen and silent, walked ahead of me now, as if getting to the dusty road was the goal of her life. That road would take us to the Tivoli road. A tractor moved along, followed by a billow of dust. Maria began to wave at the driver from among the tobacco plants and he stared at us but did not slow the tractor. Her shouts were lost in the vastness. But the driver kept his eye fixed on us, and then the tractor did begin to slow. He came to a stop. Maria began to run toward him, and it was I who was reluctant now. The cart he pulled was small and piled high with cargo. A load of dirt? I could not tell.

Maria scrambled through a gulley sweet with the smell of weeds and onto the road, where she waited for me. In her jeans she would not be mistaken for just another Italian country lass, but the dust of the field and her tousled hair lessened her look of a spoiled American.

We approached the farmer, and it was unmistakable that his load was fertilizer.

"As in shit," Maria groaned.

The driver, his body facing forward, his neck turned completely around, waited for us with an impassive expression. He wore a cloth cap, his face was weatherbeaten, and there were deep creases around his eyes. His beard looked several days old. And his undivided attention was on Maria.

"*Buon giorno,*" I said. He returned the greeting, still staring at Maria. "*Vogliamo andare per Tivoli.*"

"*Transportazione,*" Maria cried. Perhaps she felt she ought to say something, given the way he was staring at her. She babbled on in her impressionistic Italian, which the driver clearly did not understand. But then I would have sounded bookish and urban to him. My ear for the local patois was nonexistent. The language of Rome and books would be all but a foreign language to this skeptical paisano. I noticed a board in the cart that could be laid across the front to form a seat. When I indicated this to the farmer he nodded. I helped Maria up and joined her.

Thus it was that, holding our noses, riding on a load of manure, we made our way to the Tivoli road.

"Give him something," Maria suggested when we got off.

The farmer was insulted when I reached a five-thousand-lira note up to him, and I spent several minutes allowing him to establish his dignity and general indifference to the goods of this world. Then he took the money. We stood there on the blacktop road and watched him move off in the direction of Civitella.

"I need a shower," Maria said. "Ugh."

I felt the same, another motive for getting to Rome, but I intended to put Maria on a bus in Tivoli and go back to the Wilsons'. The country house and abbey, seen from the crossroads where we were, blended into a landscape that seemed a portrait of peace, but I was uneasy at the thought of Connolly there alone with Austin prowling about. The notion that Austin might mistake Connolly for me had its darker side. Maria sat on a milestone while I remained on the blacktop, ready to flag down any car that appeared. For ten minutes only one car came from the direction of Civitella, and that went by in a great roar, indifferent to my outstretched thumb.

"You give them the finger if they go by," Maria said.

"I'll remember that."

Her manner was more cheerful now. And it was pleasant at the little intersection. High above us, a hawk was being worried by smaller birds. The tractor and cart had gone out of sight when another car appeared.

"Get up here and give him a smile," I said to Maria.

She hopped up and stood beside me with a sultry expression. The approaching car seemed to slow. No wonder. It was a taxi. I flagged it down, no longer a supplicant.

We were a bonanza for the driver. He had charged his passenger from Tivoli double fare to cover his return trip, and Maria and I represented money in his pocket, more than enough to make up for the time he had spent in the taverna in Civitella.

"You drove someone from Tivoli to Civitella?"

He nodded. "Another American."

"He was young?"

"Yes."

His eyes in the rearview mirror were not on me. Like the farmer, he was fascinated by Maria. She was not unaware of this and played shamelessly to her audience of one. Thus preoccupied, she did not attach any importance to the driver's remarks.

"We smell of shit," she said to me.

"He seems to like it."

She dug me in the ribs. "Older men are crazy about me."

If I could see her only with the lusting eyes of the driver, a stranger, I would have felt her appeal again. She moved closer to me on the seat, bringing with her a redolence of the manure cart. I rolled down the window slightly.

"Don't you like my scent?"

"It smells like a million dollars."

"Boo."

It was nearly two o'clock when we arrived in Tivoli, and Maria remembered that we had not had lunch. We ate where Connolly and I had eaten after our trip to Horace's house. Maria had two quick glasses of Frascati before our food arrived, and she was in an exuberant mood.

"That was fun."

"I always keep my promises."

"Good. When is the wedding?"

I ignored that. "The ride in the cart was stupid. We could have walked as fast."

"It was a fertility symbol. I'll give you children."

Wine and romantic lack of knowledge lay behind all

this, of course. Marriage would seem only another experience to be tried, not a commitment through thick and thin. Not that it mattered. I was ineligible. And my capacity for the ridiculous was less than it had been. Maybe movie stars and millionaires can marry girls half their age, but I could not.

"The country air is getting to you. And the wine."

"Austin was really spooked when I told him."

"You told Connolly too. Don't do that, Maria. A joke is a joke, but that's going too far."

"Austin said he'll castrate you."

"Is that what you want?"

Her hand dropped on mine, and she assumed a languid expression. "What do they call a man after that?"

"Dead."

"Come on."

"Anything they want."

A eunuch for the kingdom of heaven's sake. The biblical phrase was applied to priestly celibacy. Was Maria frightened or amused by Austin? I had seen the hatred in his eyes when I fought him in Rome. I had seen the guest house after he tore it apart. I had not told Maria of the vandalism to the house and to my car. Already she was Austin's unwitting accomplice. And she was trying to make him hers, telling him of imaginary wedding plans. Did she think she could use his jealousy to spur me to a permanent arrangement?

"After we're married, Austin will just go away."

"We're not getting married."

"It doesn't have to be a religious ceremony. We can take a trip on one of those freighters you told me about and have the captain marry us."

"Austin was lurking around the Wilsons', Maria. That's why we left."

If she was surprised she did not show it. "It must have been Austin the taxi driver took out there."

He had known where to go because Maria had told him. She had whipped up his hatred by telling him we were going to get married. Was it possible that she resented me as much as I did her and dreamed of a violent end of our affair, mad Austin her instrument? All motives are mixed, I suppose, all love mixed with hate. Connolly would attribute it to Original Sin. Maybe he was right. Had it been fear for myself or worry about Maria that had prompted me to get her away from the Wilsons'? Above our table the awning flapped, and in the street debris eddied in the wind. Connolly and I had sat here talking of Horace. I wondered if the poet had harbored toward Lalage the complicated apprehension I now felt of Maria.

"I shouldn't have told Austin I'm pregnant."

"My God! You're not, are you?"

"Jim, he asks to be teased."

How menacing she seemed with her little smile, one hand on her wine glass, the other twisting her hair. Thank God she had not tried to stir a reaction from me with the claim that she was pregnant. I wondered if she had told Connolly that as well, to explain our imaginary marriage plans. In another setting I might have strangled her. Austin's fury seemed as natural as could be, there in the windswept piazza in Tivoli.

"Here is money for the bus to Rome," I said, taking lire from my pocket. "I'll pay the waiter. When you're finished, get on that bus."

"Are you going back to find Austin?" Her lips were moist with wine, and there was excitement in her eyes. Visions of gladiators clashing in the Alban hills seemed to fill her imagination.

But it was Connolly I thought of when I pushed back

from the table. The waiter came forward, and I explained that the signorina would have the meal she ordered. The amount I gave him quelled his anxiety.

"Will you be in Rome tomorrow?" Maria asked.

"I'll call you."

"At your apartment?"

Why not? I nodded, turned and went with lowered head across the piazza, the wind billowing my clothes. How I wished I were on a freighter, pacing the deck, alone, bound for anywhere at all.

Our taxi driver, full of pasta and wine, sat with his fellows across from the now closed entrance to the Villa d'Este. I told him where I wanted to go and he shook his head. Apparently his avarice had been sated by the double fare from Civitella. But when one of the other drivers showed interest, he bestirred himself. We haggled over the price on the way to his car. He insisted being paid in advance.

As we drove through the piazza I had a glimpse of Maria seated at table. Her hair drifted in the wind, but she was unbothered by it. The other diners had moved inside. Perhaps she feared her wine would be confiscated if she changed tables.

The way back seemed longer despite the harrowing speed with which the driver hurtled along the blacktop road. I was caught between wanting to beg him to slow down and to urge him on. In the middle of the back seat, grasping the handholds over the windows, I braced my knees against the front seat. My description of Austin brought inattentive nods from the driver. *Sì*. That sounded like the American he had taken to Civitella.

"You took him up to the town?"

"Yes."

"I don't want to go there."

I described where we would turn off to the Wilsons' and he slowed down. He complained that I was changing the arrangement, and my pointing out that the Wilson place was not as far as Civitella did not placate him. He did not want to leave the main road. He spoke of the narrow strip of blacktop we were on as if it were an autostrada. In the end, I offered him five thousand more if he would follow my directions to the Wilsons' gate.

"*Ladrone*," I said when we arrived.

He shrugged and pocketed the five thousand. He had turned into the Wilsons' road. Now he backed out and went off the way we had come.

As I walked toward the house, I realized how weary I was. I had spent the morning at my desk and then, without lunch, had walked miles with Maria before we caught a ride on that cart. I had had a roll and glass of wine in Tivoli. It would have been nice to feel that now I was coming home, to bathe, to rest, perhaps to swim and afterward a long aimless conversation with Connolly. It had been nice before Maria came, just the two of us, our heads full of common memories, old friends, old enemies. At least we were the same age.

How silent it was, and warm. The wind that had bothered Tivoli remained there. Perhaps the taxi had outraced it. Connolly and I together would be more than a match for Austin. If we could sit him down, we would talk some sense into him. It was silly to think of me as a rival. I was tired of pretending to be something I was not. Husband or celibate—those were ideals I could understand. I no longer wanted to sleep with empty-headed girls. Connolly and I would talk about Nancy now, at last.

When the guest house came into view, it did have the look of home, the promise of rest, somewhere I could act my age. It would be all right to tell Connolly of the mystery I had begun. He would be pleased to know I was through with his life. Furey would have to find himself another ghost. Two other ghosts.

The sound of music from the main house continued, raucous, savage, awful. But I found it reassuring. How many records had Connolly put on the turntable? I took the shortcut to the main house, jumping the little creek. When I went inside the music enveloped me like a last shrill memory of Maria. It was an ineffable pleasure to lift the arm and stop the noise. And it would alert Connolly to the fact that I was back.

When I came outside again I expected to see him on the back porch of the guest house. The door was open, but he was not standing in it. Could he have become so deafened by the music that he did not notice it had stopped?

"Michael," I called. "Mike, it's Jimmy."

It occurred to me that he could have been frightened by the stopping of the music. I did not want him to think that it was Austin who had turned it off.

Going in the door, I called his name again, questioningly. The silence was more annoying than the music had been. I went up the steps into the middle room.

Connolly was at the refectory table. One arm hung by his side, the other was outstretched, he lay face down. I approached him without awareness that I was walking. Blood from the great ugly indentation in the back of his head had flowed down his bearded cheek and onto the notebook supporting his chin. His open eye stared lifeless into eternity.

Part Four

The people gathered at the doors through which arriving passengers would come after having passed a perfunctory customs inspection grew impatient. Several represent atives of hotels and conventions held identifying signs aloft in anticipation, and free-lance cabbies skulked about awaiting their prey. It was not customs that caused the delay of the passengers on Nancy's flight, but the long wait for their baggage to begin coming in on the great U-shaped moving belt. I had caught a glimpse of Nancy and gone up to the great opaque pane of glass, cupped my hands against it, and seen her waiting wearily with the others. I knew the impatience she must feel, I had felt it so often myself. After hours in the air one ended up there, watching the belt go monotonously by as yet unburdened with luggage. I went back to the waiting crowd.

When I got back to Rome the night before, having driven nonstop from the Abbadia Celestina, my apartment had been unoccupied. Had Maria boarded the bus in Tivoli? I was sure she had. Doubtless she was up on the Monte Mario, pretending once more to be a student on her junior year in Rome. During the night I was awakened by a key in the lock. The chain prevented her from coming in. There had followed a moment of silence, then whispering. Finally the door was eased shut. She did not relock it.

By the time I came out of the bedroom and looked through the peephole, there was no one in the hall. I imagined Maria's confusion at finding the door both chained and locked. If Austin had been with her, he would have been even more confused. I locked the door from the inside.

The first trickle of passengers began to come through the doors, and those waiting pressed against the barrier, anxious to see their loved ones. Running the gamut of those welcomers, the first arrivals, wearing the washed-out look of hours in the air, of fitful sleep and too much to drink, feeling for the first time the strangeness of Rome, listened carefully to the urgent offers of the unlicensed cabbies trying to con them into a fifty-dollar ride to the city. Then the flow began in earnest. Italian, English, German and Japanese were heard, there was much milling about, and I retreated from the chaos. Let Nancy find me. A few minutes later, there she was, advancing on me as if I too bore an identifying sign.

There was a moment of hesitation when she stood before me. How does one greet a non-wife? Her eyes were puffy and the suit she wore suggested the rigors of tourist-class travel. I took her suitcase.

"Benvenuto a Roma."

She hitched up her shoulder bag and clamped her purse under her arm. "Do you have a car?"

"Right outside."

I wished I had shaken her hand at least. To kiss her would have been wrong, taking advantage of a cliché situation. She wore her hair differently from when I had seen her in Washington—it seemed even shorter—and her tired expression, her morning look, brought memories I no longer thought I had.

Outside the sun shone brightly and Nancy commented on how warm it was. I had not noticed it before. When she was settled in the passenger seat, I put her luggage in the trunk, and soon we were going through the roundabout in the center of which the massive statue of Leonardo stands, the Renaissance man of genius holding a model of one of the flying crafts he designed. When we were on the Via del Mare, I pressed down on the pedal.

Nancy said, "I had forgotten how beautiful Italy is."

"I booked a room for you at the Raphael. Do you remember it?"

She shook her head. The Hotel Raphael, vine covered, its lobby filled with unearthed antiquities, was just off the Piazza Navona, and Nancy and I had once dined in the roof garden restaurant there. Did I figure in memories of hers I did not have? The past is imperfectly parceled out among those who have shared it.

"You'll like it."

"I thought we would go to the abbey."

"You mean right away?"

"When will we go?"

"Whenever you want."

"Isn't Michael still there?"

No matter how fast I drive on the Via del Mare I am constantly being passed. Fiats went by, turn signals winking, and buses too, lemmings rushing to the sea. I looked at Nancy.

"Michael is dead."

Her lips became a line and she looked at me levelly. "No, he isn't." Her chin lifted as she turned away to stare straight ahead.

The moment of tenderness when she had stood before me after coming through the door from customs was as remote as the days of our marriage. She had made this trip to see Michael Connolly, not me. I had known that all along. But, after what had happened the day before, it was possible to imagine she was here because now Connolly was definitively dead. But of course she did not know that. Our old friend had run out of miracles. Poor Connolly. Poor Nancy too.

I lit a cigarette and we continued to Rome in silence. When I pulled up in front of the Raphael, I wondered if now she would recall the time we had been there together, but there was no sign of it. The *portiere* came out for her bags and we went through the revolving door into the lobby. While she was registering, Nancy yawned.

"I wish I weren't so tired. I slept on the plane but I hate sleeping sitting up."

"Take a nap. I'll come back for you later."

It was two o'clock in Rome, but in Washington it was nine in the morning and Nancy would feel she had been up all night.

"When?"

"Seven?"

"And tomorrow we'll go to the abbey?"

"Tomorrow we'll go to the abbey."

Why not? We crossed the lobby and I waited until the elevator doors had closed on Nancy and the *portiere* before going out to my car. Rome held no interest for Nancy. Her mind was on Michael Connolly, whom she assumed awaited us at the Abbadia Celestina. Well, she was right enough about that.

In my apartment, seated at my typewriter, trying to work up interest in my mystery, I acknowledged my disappointment. Tired as she might be, I had thought Nancy would want to see the city where we had lived, have lunch, talk. After all, she was on vacation. But it was clear it was a pilgrimage, not a vacation. Whatever expectations had been generated by Connolly's appearance at her apartment weeks before would be realized now. The expression on her face when the elevator doors closed on her was the one I had fled from when she stood in the doorway of her Washington apartment.

The phone rang and I answered it. There was half a minute of silence and then the connection was broken. Maria? Austin? How confused they must be. How could the man he killed answer his phone?

I had brought Connolly's notebook with me from the abbey. When I picked it up it was with the thought that Nancy could, by reading it, understand what had happened. But of course it did not contain the final scene. The last pages were caked with blood. Would Nancy regard it as a kind of relic?

Clark's passport does not run out for nearly three years and that means I can live in seclusion in Italy that long at least. How I wish I could stay right here. There must be some way to arrange that. The Wilsons need not know who I am. They want someone staying here when they are not using the place. But there are parties, weekend guests. I don't know. Obscurity and penance. Clark says the abbey tower reminds him of Newman Hall. I know what he means. It's odd that a minor seminary should figure so prominently in the memories of a man who did not become a priest and now claims to have lost his faith. How responsible for that am I? Nancy is sure that he suspected us years ago in Rome, that that is why he just left, resigning at *Alleluia* and not communicating with her for over a year. She's right. I know that now. Things he says. At lunch in Tivoli I thought we would speak of it at last, yet what could I have said? Words are counterfeit money. What can I do to make amends to Jimmy in this second life that has been given me? If all I did was bring him back . . .

I closed the notebook and put it in a drawer, as if I were shutting it away from Nancy's eyes. The two of them had discussed what they had done to me, knowing that I knew. I did not want his pity, if that is what it was.

The next day Nancy was unsure she remembered the abbey. We got out of the car and she looked thoughtfully at the main house, then shook her head.

"To tell you the truth, I have only the vaguest memories of the Wilsons."

"The place is different. Ian made a lot of changes."

It was not the past she sought, not our past, but Michael Connolly. When we went down to the house and I unlocked the door, she seemed to tense as she went inside. I followed her in and she wandered through the rooms as if she expected at any moment the resurrected Michael Connolly to appear and justify the long journey she had made. She did not mention him until we had gone across the lawn and up the steps to the abbey level. Looking out across the valley to Rome, she said, "He answered the phone when I called here. Michael."

"No."

She turned to me, controlling her anger. "Where did he go?"

"To heaven, I hope."

"Jim, stop it. I recognized his voice."

"Do you think he rose from the dead?"

"He wasn't on that plane! By some crazy miracle he

didn't get on it. Something convinced him he should keep it a secret. He thought talking with you would enable him to see what he should do."

"He was never in the habit of taking my advice."

"Jim, don't. Please."

I looked at the piece of plywood, anchored with a rock, and thought of the plastic bags down there. They would not interest Nancy. Why should they? She walked among the ruins of the abbey without responding to them as Connolly and I had. But then she had never been at Newman Hall, only in a Franciscan novitiate for a few months during which she had unconsciously gathered evidence against a vocation that was not hers.

"Let's look at the pool," I said.

"I want a drink."

We sat in chairs by the edge of the pool, sipping Ian's wine. It was there, an hour later, that Nancy found the interpretation she wanted.

"Jim, what if he really was on that plane?"

"He was." It was her wondrous expression that made me answer as I did.

"Think what that means."

I remembered Furey telling me about Margaret Rusher. We are surrounded by mystery. It was wrong to permit Nancy to think that a truly dead Connolly had come to talk with her in Washington. I hoped she would discard this way of making sense of what had happened. There was a sure way of forcing her to do this. I could produce the credit card charges, the notebook, invoke the witness of cabbies and waiters. Even of Maria. And there was the most definitive proof of all.

"No one will believe you," I said to Nancy.

She seemed surprised. "I don't intend to tell anyone. Jim, you mustn't either."

"I have nothing to tell."

"That's right. Forget I said anything to you."

It would be her secret, hers and St. Michael's. For the first time since she arrived in Rome, she relaxed. There was a small smile on her lips as she brought her glass to them.

"Did you love him, Nancy?"

After so many years of pretense, the question floated on the afternoon air like a deadly gas. I could not believe I had asked it. Nancy continued to look at the pool.

"I thought we both did. He was your best friend."

"That isn't what I mean."

"What do you mean?"

"Why do you think I left Rome the way I did, quit my job and everything?"

"Because you could not face up to . . ."

The death of Gregory. I got up from my chair. I had mentioned her infidelity, startling myself. I did not trust myself to keep silent about our son.

"I did love him, Jim. I still do."

I looked down at her. She sat there in slacks and blouse, a pair of sunglasses pushed up on her head, a glass of wine in her hand. Her words annulled our marriage as no court could. I nodded. I was not even angry. The truth shall set you free.

"You were always jealous of him, Jim."

"I never aspired to be a theologian."

"You were always picking arguments with him, taking positions you didn't believe in, opposing him."

"That's true."

"Why?"

"You said it. I was jealous."

"Is that why you agreed to write a book about him, revenge?"

"I've dropped that."

"Good."

I delivered Michael Connolly into her possession. She would not tell anyone he had come to her apartment after he died. It was something she wanted to keep to herself, to cherish. In that at least she was different from Furey.

"I'm going for a walk. Do you want more wine?"

"No."

In the cloister, hands behind my back, I paced as monks had paced centuries before. I felt at peace. I thought of Gregory and did not try to prompt myself to tears. My son was better off where he was. Later, I went down to the nave and through the arched opening in the ruined wall and looked down at the spot where I had buried Connolly, bringing his body in a wheelbarrow from the guest house under cover of darkness. But it is never wholly dark.

It is a solemn thing to dig a grave and bury an old friend. It would have been too complicated if I had called the police. After all, Connolly had died once before. And been buried too. Austin? The demands of justice seemed unimportant to me. When I was done, I stood beside the grave and, as Muscat had, began the "De profundis." Like Muscat, I could not finish the psalm. It did not seem to matter. It was right that Connolly should lie here, as anonymous as the monks in the plastic bags. He had wanted to stay here and his prayer had been answered.

The grave did not look like a grave. My efforts to disguise it were more successful than I had thought. There was little danger that it would be discovered. Connolly could rest in peace. I tried to think of him as nothing more than a memory, persisting for a while in the brains of those who had known him and ultimately disappearing completely when they did. But he seemed as real as Nancy and myself.

From the fresco on the refectory walls, the wide unblinking eyes of the fading Christ looked down at me. I stopped and met his gaze. Remember how our hearts burned within us when we walked with him on the way. It seemed a mockery to permit Nancy to think that Connolly had appeared to her after his death. I ran no risk by telling her what had really happened. I had lost whatever love she had for me long ago. The trouble was she already knew what had really happened. Her credulity was willful, a parody of faith. The fresco vouchsafed no help.

I went down the steps and across the lawn to the pool and Nancy and one damned thing after another.

Ralph McInerny has written several novels, including *The Priest*, which find their themes in the groves of academe and the often comic, sometimes tragic, commotion that plagues the post-conciliar Church. He is also the author of the very popular Father Dowling mystery series.

Since 1955 McInerny has taught at the University of Notre Dame where he is Michael P. Grace Professor of Medieval Studies and Director of both the Medieval Institute and the Jacques Maritain Center.